HORSEBACK GOVERNMENT

Ad Interim Administration
Republic of Texas 1836

Also by the author:

State Shapes — U.S.A. Visual Aid

HORSEBACK GOVERNMENT

Ad Interim Administration
Republic of Texas 1836

by Ruth Juby Carnes

The Naylor Company
Book Publishers of the Southwest
San Antonio, Texas

Library of Congress Cataloging in Publication Data

Carnes, Ruth Juby, 1914-
    Horseback government; ad interim administration, Republic of Texas, 1836.

    Bibliography: p.
    1. Texas—History—Revolution, 1835-1836—Fiction.
I. Title.
PZ4.C2876Ho3   [PS3553.A754]   813'.5'4   74-3188
ISBN 0-8111-0521-0

TO MY CRAIN COMETS
Of yesterday — today — and hopefully, tomorrow

Contents

Introduction   ix
Wednesday: March 16, 1836   1
Thursday: March 17, 1836 — From Midnight On . . .   6
Friday: March 18, 1836   13
Saturday: March 19, 1836   18
Sunday: March 20, 1836   22
Monday: March 21, 1836   28
Tuesday: March 22, 1836   34
Wednesday: March 23, 1836   38
Thursday: March 24, 1836   42
Friday: March 25, 1836   45
Saturday: March 26, 1836   47
Sunday: March 27, 1836   51
Monday: March 28, 1836   53
Tuesday: March 29, 1836   56
Wednesday: March 30, 1836   58
Thursday: March 31, 1836   62
Friday: April 1, 1836   63
Saturday: April 2, 1836   65
Sunday: April 3 — Saturday: April 9, 1836   66
Sunday: April 10, 1836   72
Monday: April 11, 1836   72
Tuesday: April 12, 1836   73
Wednesday: April 13, 1836   74

Thursday: April 14, 1836   77
Friday: April 15, 1836   78
Saturday: April 16, 1836   81
Sunday: April 17, 1836   83
Monday: April 18, 1836   88
Tuesday: April 19, 1836   90
Wednesday: April 20, 1836   93
Thursday: April 21, 1836   94
Friday: April 22, 1836   98
Saturday: April 23, 1836   106
Sunday: April 24, 1836   108
Monday: April 25, 1836   109
Later   111
The Seven Men on Horseback (chart)   115
Texas Declaration of Independence   116
Bibliography   124

Illustrations on pages 122 and 123

Introduction

It was the students in one of my Texas history classes a few years back that are responsible for my writing this book. Their desire to learn more about the Texas Revolution than the textbook gave them started me on my search for additional materials.

Their interest plunged me deeper into the project than I ever expected. It continued to compel me toward libraries, museums, memorial parks, and monuments long after they had left my classroom.

Remember the Alamo, Remember Goliad, Victory at San Jacinto — have been imprinted upon our hearts, and justly so. Names such as Houston, Travis, Crockett, Bowie, and Fannin, along with others, are found on many pages in the annals of Texas history.

But seldom did I find anything about the Ad Interim Government of the Republic, which is also called the Horseback Government; nor our first president, David Gouverneur Burnet — and his fellow officers, Lorenzo de Zavala, Samuel P. Carson, Bailey Hardeman, Thomas J. Rusk, Robert Potter, and David Thomas.

They are the unsung heroes who have almost been lost in the shuffle down through the years. Few know of their worthy contributions, though they were equally as important as our military heroes.

Under the most trying circumstances, the government was run from the saddle of the president's sweat-lathered horse, with Santa Anna hot on his heels. The dictator's determination to capture these men — most especially Zavala, who was a mortal enemy — finally led him to his downfall.

Plans were made as the officers galloped from place to place. There was no time for writing formal minutes on this wild flight, and perhaps bulging saddlebags — which contained the Declaration of Independence and the Constitution, along with other valuables — would not have held them anyway.

Consequently, information has been hard to come by. Thank goodness for the handbills, proclamations, etc., that have been preserved in the Archives of the Texas State Library, and the Barker Library on The University of Texas campus.

It became a game with me to collect bits and pieces of information that were scattered here, there, and everywhere, as to what these men did in the cause of freedom. This went on for months and my collection became voluminous. Books, magazine clippings, and scads of Xeroxed copies were stacked or stashed away all around the house — even under the bed. It was when I began to assemble this jumble of facts into a more orderly manner that I decided to write *Horseback Government*.

I have told it like it really was on a day-by-day basis, taking the liberty to interject the way I believe these gallant men felt about themselves and each other in their struggle to keep the new nation together. If others gain a more complete picture of the Texas Revolution, because of my having done so, I shall feel justly rewarded.

I am indeed indebted to many writers of history. I have drawn heavily from the works of such noted historians as Eugene C. Barker, Col. William F. Gray (bless him for his prejudiced diary), Mary Austin Holley, Louis W. Kemp, Walter Prescott Webb, plus many others. A complete list is given in the bibliography.

Too, I shall always be eternally grateful to my husband, Hubert Carnes, who has stood by and given me many words of encouragement during these past few months.

And to those wonderful librarians — I also give my most sincere thanks.

Wednesday: March 16, 1836

The tragic news of the fall of the Alamo was finally confirmed that morning at the Texas capital in Washington-on-the-Brazos. People gathered in the village on the west bank of the Brazos River (opposite the mouth of the Navasota River) seeking to know all each man could tell another.

The bitter and inescapable truth about the death of all its defenders could no longer be suppressed, not even by Gen. Sam Houston. It was so. William B. Travis, James Bowie, David Crockett with his "Tennessee Boys," and all the rest had been put to the sword ten days before.

Messengers galloped in with many tales of horror. Each report had been more disheartening than the last. The news passed from one to another of how Gen. Antonio de Santa Anna, president of Mexico and commander of its military forces, was sweeping this way to wipe out the rest of the rebels. Most agreed they'd best take up arms to avenge their fallen heroes.

Men of all ages, even fuzzy-cheeked boys, were strapping muzzle loaders and squirrel guns on their saddles and rushing off to join the army. Frantic women gathered their children together and started eastward, hoping to get away from the Mexicans before it was too late.

Delegates to the Constitutional Convention were called into a late session at ten o'clock. Little had been accomplished during the day, other than read communiques and send out spies to spot the enemy. To try to settle the controversial loan and land problems now was out of the question. All they could possibly hope for in this state of confusion was to polish off the Constitution and to accept it for better or for worse.

It had been a long hot day for the members. And a swig from the jug by a few hadn't helped to cool things down any. They had heated arguments that wound up into fights and brawls over the way Richard Ellis, chairman of the convention from Red River bottom, was handling things.

Ellis had been unable to keep the prejudices of the Governor-Council fight (an earlier government) from filtering into the meetings. They accused him of picking his cronies to serve on more than one committee; of ignoring the rest of them with his go-to-hell attitude; of being in the pocket of the loan sharks; of leaning toward "fat cat" land speculators; and of breaking up the convention tonight if it didn't go his own selfish way. It was a gamble as to how this meeting would go.

All of this and more hung heavy over their heads as they made their way with lighted lanterns through the darkened street, avoiding trees and stumps and stones. Beside them were squatty log cabins and

2

a few frame buildings, along with many horses tied up to posts on a campground that was crowded to capacity. Dying campfires silhouetted tents and wagons from every part of Texas. The screech of an owl, a baby's cry, and the mournful howl of a coyote reverberating through the trees added to the uneasiness that hung over the valley.

Off by itself, as befitted a building of such importance, was Independence Hall; it was less than a quarter of a mile from the bluffs. The long, narrow, gun-barrel type building with a high-pitched roof had been hastily slapped together out of raw boards. It was still not finished — no windows or door at the opening, and only temporary steps. It did have a floor, though, of rough-hewn planks.

The hall was crowded. It was hot and stuffy. Canvas on the windows was propped back for air. A makeshift table, topped with documents and lighted lanterns, had been pushed back against the wall. Latecomers heaved their sweaty bodies in through the ranks, shoving and pushing the next one for a place to stand; the doorkeeper didn't have a chance at checking credentials. They were all talking at once, raising their voices to the rafters. Tension mounted like hot steam from a kettle.

Richard Ellis stared at the throng of muttering people through the light of the flickering lanterns. He was slowly rising to his feet in an effort to get on with the meeting. He pulled out his pistol that was strapped around his middle and placed it upon the table. Then he lifted a hand for silence. The ranting crowd paid him no heed. He tapped sharply upon the table but he still could not make himself heard.

He clenched his fists, fire rising in his voice, and shouted; but he could not calm the overwrought

3

group. His voice mounted till he was screaming and his face red with anger. The hall rocked with shouts and sneers. People went crazy, wild screaming crazy.

The man had had it — he was through. He took a deep breath and like a lightning flash on a dark night, he thundered out, "The meeting is adjourned. We'll retreat to Nacogdoches — and start over."

Then he picked up his pistol, turned on his heels, and made for the door like a bull charging a red flag; and his cohorts went rushing after him. They were deserting like rats on a sinking ship.

A stocky man in a jaunty black suit was bracing himself against the vanishing crowd. It was Judge David Gouverneur Burnet, a native of New Jersey who had stopped off from Harrisburg as a visitor at the convention a few days before; he had previously planned to continue on to the Alamo in answer to Travis' plaintive pleas for help.

Revolt was nothing new to the bearded, middle-aged man with a shock of heavy hair, piercing eyes, and a face like it was carved from Texas stone. As an orphan and a restless teen-ager, he had sailed with revolutionaries into South America where he fired the first shot for freedom against the Spanish conquerors.

He had learned to use the tomahawk and knife like a warrior from the Comanche tribe in Texas — which was long before Stephen F. Austin had brought his "Old Three Hundred" in. He had crossed the country with the Bible in one hand and a pistol in the other. But for all this he was a kind and gentle man who had held out for a peaceful settlement with Mexico until the very last.

Burnet's mouth stiffened into a thin line as he caught a glimpse of Richard Ellis. How he would

4

like to ram those fateful words back down that man's throat. He couldn't stomach the thoughts of moving to Nacogdoches; and a sick feeling ran up and down his body.

He broke out in a cold sweat on his forehead and in his palms. He reeled from the heat. He scarcely knew where he was. Then piece by piece things came back. Suddenly he knew what he must do.

He must convince the people to stay. They had to have a government — now. It would be too late, once they scattered to the four winds. It wouldn't be easy for him as words usually didn't come out the way he intended. Somehow he made his way to the top of a shaky bench, striving to keep his balance and endure the stifling heat.

"Who's that?" someone called out.

Others turned back. "Why that's Burnet!" they said. Burnet was known all over Texas as a former empresario and a judge who dealt out justice under shady oaks for the poor and oppressed.

People stopped. The light on their faces showed them dazed and unable to take in what was happening. But Burnet could tell by the way they were drifting back that they were ready to listen.

A shocked murmur arose — some shouts of protest. But Burnet paid them no heed. He stood tall as a mighty oak and didn't budge an inch. He might be axed after this but he wasn't about to give in now.

"Are you of a mind to give up your freedom?" he spoke out in a smooth, throaty voice.

"No-o-o," they answered, crowding closer.

"I'm here to ask you to stay. I know it's a sudden sounding thing and — "

There was still some protesting but he kept on pouring oil over the troubled waters. He told them

5

time was running out; that they must stand together and put their shoulders to the wheel for Texas. He told about the Mexicans — the Alamo in flames — patriots burning on the funeral pyre. He reminded them of the Declaration of Independence that they had signed on March 2 and what it stood for.

When he had finished he stepped down weak and numb with exhaustion. Men wrung his hand and pounded his shoulders joyfully. Richard Ellis had a hangdog look. All knew it hadn't been easy for him to stay and listen. But he, too, ambled up and offered his hand. Burnet knew he'd made his mark.

Lorenzo de Zavala, friend-turned-foe of the mighty Santa Anna, spoke in perfect English urging the delegates to act at once. Then Samuel Price Carson made a similar appeal. And Richard Ellis called the undisciplined — though nonetheless patriotic — delegates back into session. In an orderly manner befitting the rising nation, they accepted and adopted the Constitution shortly after the stroke of twelve o'clock midnight.

Thursday: March 17, 1836
— From Midnight On . . .

The laws of the new nation rang like an echo from the past patterned largely after the Constitution of the United States. The document, however, could not actually become official until it was submitted to the people and confirmed by a majority vote. There was no time left for that.

So an ordinance was passed sometime after midnight to organize an Ad Interim (temporary) government. In reality this was the beginning of a Horseback Government, as you shall soon find out.

No less than a half-dozen candidates had unofficially thrown their hats in the ring for the presidential race. Houston was not included as he was in the wilderness rounding up troops and making peace with the Indians. Neither was Stephen Austin, who was in the states trying to get aid. It is doubtful that they would have been favored had they been there.

Behind-the-scenes deals and wrangling had been going on since the start of the convention. Finally they had reached a point where there was no possible chance of agreeing or carrying a majority for any one candidate. There was only one other thing left for them to do — look for a dark horse candidate whom all could agree upon.

At that moment the names of David G. Burnet and Samuel P. Carson — both late arrivals on the scene — were placed up for consideration. The votes were counted; and like a bright star in the darkening sky, the name of DAVID GOUVERNEUR BURNET came blazing forth.

After the election of Burnet as president the dam was broken. Emotional strains drained away and it became only a matter of routine to select the rest of the official family. With the knowledge and consent of the new president, all officers were unanimously elected. They were all delegates to the convention, Burnet being the only one who was not.

Let's meet them:

LORENZO DE ZAVALA — the suave, Spanish-speaking son of the Yucatán jungle — was the vice-president. This little man of dark skin with neatly clipped sideburns and snappy brown eyes had made a big name for himself in the annals of Mexican history: politics, democratic reforms, medicine, writing, language linguistics, plus his recent, ill-fated appointment by General Santa Anna as minister of Mexico to France.

At this time, in his late forties, he was a voluntary exile from his mother country with a price that hung heavy over his head. Now, from near Harrisburg, he joined hands with the Texans to help put an end to the tyrannical reign of a ruthless despot.

SAMUEL PRICE CARSON, secretary of state, could have easily been a playboy in his time. He was smart, good looking, popular and a rich planter's son in North Carolina. But he strived to do his best — whether it be leading the gospel singing at a camp meeting, fighting a duel to avenge his father's good name, or stumping the state for votes in political campaigns.

Carson had driven himself so hard in politics — both state and national — that he looked much older than his thirty-eight years. He arrived at Peach Point up near the Red River the previous spring and was one of five to represent this area.

BAILEY HARDEMAN was picked as secretary of the treasury, though there was no money for him to keep. When seventeen he marched from the hills of Tennessee to fire a cannon for Andrew Jackson in the War of 1812. Now, at forty-one, he was a lawyer, residing in Matagorda Municipality since the previous fall; he was accompanied to Texas by his brother Thomas.

THOMAS JEFFERSON RUSK, the secretary

of war, was from South Carolina. He studied law under famous statesmen of the day and passed the bar at an early age. The slender, clean-shaven man of thirty-two would be again reunited with his friend, Gen. Sam Houston, in the mustering of troops and supplies for the Revolutionary army.

When he settled down the year before in Nacogdoches Municipality he was broke, busted, and disgusted. He had chased some swindlers all the way to Texas who had beaten him out of a lot of money. He found them but it was too late; they had squandered and gambled it away.

When ROBERT POTTER was selected as secretary of the navy, there was some question. The slender, quick-tempered politician with steely black eyes had a notorious past; besides, he was picked as a delegate for Nacogdoches — at the point of a gun — by some latecomers from the United States, rather than by the established settlers. However, since the thirty-six-year-old North Carolinian had also been a midshipman, they agreed that he was the one to chart the course for the navy.

DAVID THOMAS was the attorney general. Little is known about him, other than he was a lawyer, single at thirty-five, and a Tennessee rover who had come with a loaded gun ready to fight. He was also chosen (like Potter) by those new volunteers from the states to represent Refugio.

A swearing-in ceremony was held for these new officers of the Horseback Government, with Richard Ellis administering the oath. He shook their hands, wished them godspeed, and placed the gavel in the hands of Pres. David G. Burnet.

President Burnet stood alone now behind the lectern. This was his special moment. He swept a shock of unruly hair from his sweaty forehead, and with a shine in his eyes, delivered the inaugural address. There was pride and confidence in the way he spoke out; and the tired founding fathers were with him from the first words of hope down to the last bit of advice for the trying days ahead.

One by one the people groped out at four o'clock in the morning to find their cots and pallets. They had labored some seventeen days and nights. And many a time it looked as they would never accomplish what they had started out to do. Their wide differences of opinion could be readily understood, since they had come from all points of the compass; moreover, the fifty-nine members represented various walks of life — many farmers, some lawyers, a few doctors and a Methodist minister.

But somehow they had managed to list their grievances against Mexico and make a final break for freedom in the Declaration of Independence, set up some rules in the Constitution, and select Sam Houston as their general; and now they had elected some trusted men to carry on for the newborn nation. This they had done in the midst of the enemy (not to mention hostile Indians) without any protection. All fit together like pieces in a puzzle.

They were proud and somewhat relieved, though each knew full well there was more to freedom than this. And many a one prayed in the darkness for guidance to see them through.

Back at the hall, Burnet called his cabinet together for a short session. They polished off the Constitution and journal to take to the printers down at San Felipe, discussed how to stop panic and raise money, then made plans for the morning session, which had been called for nine o'clock.

After a few hours of sleep and a good breakfast, the patriots drifted in for the first meeting of the Republic of Texas. It seemed as if all was moving along quite smoothly: They approved the rules for importing goods; waved the go-ahead sign to issue treasury notes, though they were unsecured; made plans to feed and clothe the refugees as much as possible; and then passed the buck on the loan-and-land problem onto the new officers.

President Burnet issued a proclamation that they would move the capital to Harrisburg. This came as no great surprise as there had been some talk about this during the earlier part of the night. It would be much easier to communicate there with the United States, among other reasons.

Suddenly there was a disturbance outside — a horse's whinny, clacking of hoofs, and a loud yell. An uneasiness rippled through the crowd like a breeze through rows of growing corn. They turned their heads toward the door. Some from the back went to see what was the matter.

Then a strange rider on a sweat-lathered horse called out in a high shrill voice as he passed the hall, "The Mexicans are coming! The Mexicans are coming!"

That struck the people dumb. Burnet saw cold shock stiffen their faces. They had no protection. Gonzales was in flames; Sam Houston had thrown his cannon in the river and fled. His little army was, no doubt, miles away. They had waited too long.

Then a man called out, "Remember the Alamo!"

And that did it. The hall rocked with the chant. They were trapped in the mounting pressures. There wasn't any time to waste. Every minute brought the

Mexicans closer. President Burnet, sensing the urgency of the situation, adjourned the meeting.

The patriots saddled up and went pounding off in all directions — some to check on their families, while others turned toward the army. But their fast getaway was no match for the speed of the loan sharks. They were the first to light a shuck out of there in nothing flat.

The sky was a gloomy gray and threatening storm clouds were hanging low over the village. Burnet was saddened as he looked at the procession which history has tagged as the "Runaway Scrape." He wondered if he would ever be able to hold them together long enough for victory. He thought of his wife and two young children; he feared for their safety.

Then he turned his thoughts toward his country. No doubt about that alarm — Santa Anna *was* headed this way. He was probably crossing the Colorado River at that time. This would be some sixty miles away, so he reasoned it would be several days before the arrival.

And a sudden thought flashed through Burnet's mind. He whirled around toward his fellow officers and asked, "Do you suppose Santa Anna has been tipped off that Lorenzo is here?"

After much discussion, it was decided that Lorenzo de Zavala, the vice-president, must disguise and leave immediately. The Mexican patriot threw a halter on a flea-bitten mule and took off towards his home. He lived near the new capital so he would be ready for them when they arrived.

Also, Sam Carson, Bailey Hardeman, and David Thomas took to the saddle, since they would not be especially needed here. They headed for Jared Groce's plantation to lay plans for a stay-over there.

12

David Burnet, Thomas Rusk, and Robert Potter remain. Since Rusk was the secretary of war, he was to be responsible for directing traffic down at Groce's Ferry; also, to scrounge for men, horses, and supplies there. Potter offered his assistance, wherever it was needed.

Burnet started a proclamation aimed at residents of the Red River area. There was some doubt within his mind as to whether these people would follow through or not.

Darkness fell on the desolated village and rain was pelting down. Burnet pulled his black coat to, as if protecting his tired body, then hunched over as he stepped out into the drenching rain. He thought to himself, "Well, at least this will slow Santa Anna down a bit — and give us a little more time."

Friday: March 18, 1836

It was a gloomy morning in Washington-on-the-Brazos. The dense fog had turned into a steady drizzle. Pres. David Burnet, Secretary of War Thomas Rusk, and Secretary of the Navy Robert Potter were seeing the remaining people off.

By afternoon the village had become a ghost town. All was quiet and still. Only the bellow of bullfrogs and the distant caw of a crow broke the eerie stillness. Even the Spanish moss, which hung in drippy festoons from the oaks, had taken on a ghastly appearance.

It was time for the three officials to go. They mounted up with official papers packed in their sad-

13

dlebags. Their spirits were dampened and fears of the unknown crept in as they slowly cut their ruts southward.

Burnet took a long last look behind him. He spotted Independence Hall. True, it was no great capitol; yet it looked so quiet and peaceful and dignified up there. He wondered if he would ever see it again.

He faced forward with renewed courage and determination as he rode on with his fellow officers toward Groce's Ferry. They followed the contour of the Brazos River, which was rising steadily due to the heavy rains along its upper branches in the western plains. No doubt it would soon spill over somewhere before having to give itself up to the Gulf of Mexico.

The Brazos is the longest river in Texas and it flows through the richest land in the country. The farmers were indeed fortunate that the stream was deep enough to accommodate steamboats for transporting their products down to the Gulf.

The river has as many names as it has tributaries. Old settlers called its upper branches the Salt Forks; there was actually enough salt in it during the dry months to pickle their pork.

The Indians had been calling the river Tokonohono for many moons and featured it in colorful red picture writings upon stones along its cliffs. Early explorers also had their own names for it, depending upon the season and what place they discovered it.

The Spaniards found the river while searching for gold and called it El Rio de los Brazos de Dios, or The River of the Arms of God; perhaps this was because it quenched their thirst on a hot summer day. A swashbuckling Frenchman named La Salle hap-

14

pened upon the river when it was on a rampage much like today and called it the Maligne, which means the wicked one.

But none of that was on the minds of the three horsemen now. All they were thinking about was how to cross it. For by the time they had reached the ferry, it had been stopped.

The ferryman told the men there was no way to cross the tempestuous river, that it was not a stream to be reckoned with when it gets on a rage such as this.

Robert Potter, daredevil of the navy, spoke up, "Why can't we put up a barricade?"

The ferryman said it would be disastrous and that he wanted no part of it. He mentioned that he wouldn't give a thin dime for their lives if they tried it.

"We're a bunch of damn fools to try it," Rusk said, as he looked at the red, swollen waters. "We'll all end up strumming a harp."

Then he turned to his leader. Burnet studied a long moment and strode up and down the bank. He knew what it meant to cross a river like this. But he also knew that if they didn't make that crossing now it might be too late for a Texas government.

Then he looked the two squarely in the face. "Well, we may go down to the muddy bottom, but we must take our chances."

The two nodded their agreement. They dragged logs out into the current to make it swirl toward the opposite bank, then slid their horses down the slippery banks into the red, churning waters. They dodged trees and branches and long pieces of timber; they bobbled up and down like little corks on a fishing pole.

15

But somehow they made it to the other side. "By the grace of God," said Burnet, "we're here." He pressed his Bible closer to his heart.

They kept on, drenched to the skin, along the trail beside plantations that were planted in cotton and corn. These planters stood to lose more financially than any other group in the Republic, unfortunately. The largest owner was Jared Groce, who was to be their host that night.

Their approach to the plantation did not especially appeal to Burnet, even though he was worn and weary and wet. The thoughts of Groce left a bad taste in his mouth. He thought of him as a "slick one," who was supposed to have traded a hank of cloth and a horse for a whole town, lock, stock and barrel.

They arrived well after dark, following the gleam of the lighted window up to the great house. Mr. Groce met the dejected trio at the door with a wry smile. "Hallo — light and hitch," he said. "Been looking for you — Carson told me you were coming."

Burnet was mildly surprised to find the land and loaners there, too; he didn't reckon they were there to spread any oil on the troubled waters. But he was not for deciding that night, not for sour apples. No doubt the Republic was in desperate straits for money, but they needed more time to think things through.

After a hearty supper, the tired but determined officials talked about the Republic's problems. There were five members in attendance — Bailey Hardeman was missing as he was well on his way home by then, and Zavala was hid out in the underbrush somewhere between here and Washington-on-the-Brazos.

They discussed such weighty subjects as: agents to go to the United States to seek recognition for the Republic, which would make it legal to ask for aid;

and payment to T. F. McKinney, a merchant from Quintana, for supplies already received from him — they could draw a draft of $10,000 on the bank at New Orleans, which had been deposited by Stephen F. Austin and his committee.

Since there was no seal for Carson — the secretary of state — to stamp official papers with, they appointed one of his friends to design one; the provisional government prior to this one had used the imprint of a coat button, which was centered with a starlike design.

Too, Burnet had finished and issued the following proclamation to the doubting East Texans:

> The enemy is advancing upon our borders, their hands still warm with the blood of our gallant brothers slaughtered in the Alamo.
>
> In the name of Texas I exhort you Citizens of Red River to repair with alacrity to the field, and to chastise the audacity of the Invader. Your brothers of the sea coast and the interior are in arms, and we confidently rely on our ability to sustain this portion of the Republic. The enemy threatens us with a speedy conquest and conquest by such an enemy, imports an indiscriminate extermination.
>
> Citizens of Texas! Your all is at stake. Your wives; your children, all that is dear and sacred to free men summon you to the field. Your inherent gallantry will promptly obey the call. Texas in this hour of her extremity, needs the aid of every citizen: let none prove recreant and all will prosper.

The enemy knows and dreads your prowess. They depend on numbers, *we* on the justice of our cause, the approbation of our God, and a high pre-eminance of National character. Citizens of Red River! The war in which you have a common interest with all Texas, has hitherto been conducted without you — It now devolves upon you to bear a portion of its burdens. Your patriotism is not doubted, your courage and ability are fully appreciated by your fellow citizens. Let the enemy experience the one and feel the other. One bold united exertion of our strength — conducted with skill, will bring the contest to a speedy and glorious termination; and peace, fortune and independence are certain results.[1]

Saturday: March 19, 1836

It seemed to David Burnet and his cabinet like they had barely closed their eyes when daylight came. With aching bones they piled out of bed and made ready for the busy day ahead. They walked outside along the gravelled walk to get out of hearing distance of the loaners; too, they were looking the place over as it was to be the temporary capitol for the next few days.

They had accepted Jared Groce's invitation to stay over so they could get the government better

1 Sloan, Sallie Everett, "The Presidential Administration of David G. Burnet," March 17-October 22, 1836, The University of Texas, Austin, Texas, June 1918, pp. 21-23.

organized. It was with reluctance that Burnet agreed to this as he did not want to be obligated to any man, now; but he was in no position to reject the offer, since the other folks in the valley were smaller farmers and could not afford such accommodations.

Groce had built this plantation high upon the tree-shadowed slope only three years before and dubbed it "The Retreat." He said it was his way of getting away from malaria fever, which was so prevalent in the Brazos bottoms. Though this might have lessened the chills and fever somewhat, it did little to cut down on the armies of mosquitoes that seemed to follow him.

The long roomy house had a spacious front porch, which was supported with great round columns. Tall chimneys stood like giant smokestacks on both sides. Many lesser buildings were clumped together around toward the back, giving further evidence of prosperity to the landscape. There were cabins for the slaves — that was legal then — and other buildings, such as a blacksmith shop, smokehouses, and corncribs.

"Not bad," said Tom Rusk, as he viewed the surroundings, and spotted their horses grazing on the grassy meadow. Then he turned toward the president. "But how are we going to handle the loan situation, Dave?"

"Yes," Robert Potter chimed in, "those money bags are going to be up and at us today."

Burnet was not known as one to make up his mind right away, especially now — since he wondered just how sincere some of these men were. He had a habit of looking up and twisting his head sideways, as if he was seeking higher help before answering. In this stance, he thought of the time when he was seventeen and had lost all his inheritance trying to

19

save someone whom he trusted very much. This had had a tendency on him to be leary of deals which involved money.

Finally, after reflecting, he got around to saying, "We must do what is best for Texas and not for any one individual."

"But, Boss," said Rob Potter, who was known for making snap judgments, "let's get it over with and send them on their way."

"I'm with Rob," said David (Davy) Thomas. The attorney general was quick on the draw like Rob Potter and was eager to start reeling off legal advice to the rest of the members. "These men are rolling fat in money and Texas doesn't have a thin dime, except that little dribble Austin managed to bank in New Orleans."

Burnet put in, "But you must remember the government before us thought Austin and his men paid too dearly for what they got and blocked it. You recall Austin gave the lenders an option to take choice land at the rate of fifty cents an acre for repayment of the loan."

Tom Rusk spoke up, "I'm a little dubious of some of these men." You will recall that he too had reason to doubt when it came to money matters because of those so-called "honest" ones who took him for his cash back east in his home state of South Carolina. "How do we know who to trust?"

After talking back and forth, they decided, as they turned toward the house, to play it by ear until they could weigh all the facts that were to be presented. The process of elimination might not be a bad idea.

And that is just what they did. The members of the cabinet listened to the tough and determined businessmen who were seeking profit and choice lands

20

for the least amount of investment — some under the veil of patriotism. At times it was very hard to keep from blowing their tops, especially so for Rob Potter.

Burnet knew that he needed these men and he bent over backwards to hear each one out. He sat in his chair and from all appearances it seemed as if he was calm, cool, and collected. But he was in a turmoil within. It was as if half of him wanted to erupt, while the other half was pushing him down.

Finally, toward the end of the day, he thanked them in as tactful a way as he was able to muster, and with the consent of the cabinet, he announced the matter would be tabled for further study.

"Good going, David," said Tom Rusk, as he leaned over to Burnet. "I say give some of them enough rope and they'll hang themselves."

"Thank you, Tom," whispered Burnet.

Needless to say the capitalists were aghast. A few did leave in a huff and some threatened to go; but most of them stayed. The shrewd ones as well as those sincere to the duties of their country knew that, sooner or later, there would be a showdown and they aimed to be around when it happened.

Aside from this hot issue, word was received that the Mexicans had the Indians to the east on the warpath; that many a redskin was fitting his bow to the arrow ready to pluck off the white man. They deputized Michel B. Menard, a former French fur trader and a declaration signer, as an Indian agent — giving him two thousand dollars for presents to keep the Indians happy.

Messengers and an aide-de-camp, as well as scouts and secretaries for the government, were selected. Requests from late arrivals for commissions were given consideration.

21

Meanwhile — Gen. Sam Houston and his motley crew, who wore clothes of buckskin or homespun and carried every weapon imaginable — are still retreating down the east bank of the Colorado River, across from Beasons; this is near where Columbus is now. They were to wait there for artillery and reinforcements. Whence cometh their help — only the man upstairs could tell.

Col. James W. Fannin, at the request of General Houston, pulled out of Goliad in a fog that morning headed for Victoria. He could foresee no special reason to hurry, so took his time destroying surplus commodities before leaving out. But he tarried too long and got caught off out in the open prairie, away from food and water. He was surrounded by Gen. José Urrea and his Mexican army by nightfall. Why a supposedly brilliant man, trained in West Point Academy, would use such military strategy as this is indeed hard to understand.

Sunday: March 20, 1836

The president and his four cabinet members who were at Groce's were making ready to push on toward Harrisburg the next day. President Burnet sat hunched over the table rereading the Declaration of Independence. The document, which would soon be stashed away in his saddlebags with other very important papers, was written in longhand upon crumpled parchment. Even at that it was on better paper than the journal reports were; those pages made you think that they might have been torn from one of our grade school tablets.

His eyes stopped when they got to where it read about freedom of religion — "it denies us the right of worshipping the Almighty according to the dictates of our own conscience. . . ."

The day being Sunday, he was ever mindful of the fact that still no church bells (save those of the Roman Catholic) would be ringing in Texas that morning. If another service was held, it would be within the wall of some log cabin with sentries posted outside.

Most of the settlers were Protestants but many had given lip service to the Catholic religion in order to obtain land, which was the main reason they had come in the first place. When a man took the vows, not only did he agree to become a Catholic but a citizen of the Republic of Mexico as well. And if he married a Mexican señorita he would be given even more land; a few also did this.

David Burnet was one of the few who had bowed his neck and refused to be baptized again; also he would not permit a priest to remarry him. He had been married by a Presbyterian minister at Morristown, New Jersey and that was good enough for him.

He had paid dearly for this denial though. They cancelled the grant which he was to have received for operating a sawmill; according to Mexican law, an empresario was to be given an additional amount of land if he supplied extra services such as this to the people.

This was a bitter blow to an ambitious man, just married at forty-two, who was eager to make a new start in this big, beautiful country. His mind wandered to the problems they had had getting that steam engine here. They had chartered a boat to bring the machinery and some families to help him operate it, along with furnishings for their new home.

All had gone well until just before their arrival, when they hit a storm just off the coast of Galveston. They were grounded. They worked frantically day and night trying to break loose but the ship wouldn't budge. Finally, as a last resort, they had to throw all the extras overboard.

He could see his beautiful bride, Hannah, now as they threw her new furniture over, along with her hope chest, that contained her wedding gown and many hand-sewn pieces, which she had been adding to ever since she was big enough to thread a needle.

He remembered she did not cry. She just stared, her face as pale as a sheet, when she saw her treasures sink down to the briny deeps. The despairing look in her eyes haunted him to this day.

And finally they had lost the sawmill, too. He was in such dire straits that he sold it last year at a tremendous loss. He had sunk practically all he had into the project — money from the sale of a former contract to the Galveston Bay and Texas Land Company (retaining only a small interest), plus what he could rake and scrape together from his law practice.

He could not keep from wondering how it might have been, had he given up his own religion and worshipped in their way. He shook his head and thought, "No, I'm no hypocrite. I'll stand true to my faith and my ideals until I die."

He glanced out the window. The wind was blowing restlessly. Trees shook like they were trembling. He gazed down at the strange caravan of carts, wagons, horses, or what-have-you conveyances, as they squished along the trail. The ferry had reopened, now that the river had gone down some, and those that had been stranded on the other side were hastening to catch up with the others.

Over at the hitching post, he spotted Vice-Pres. Lorenzo de Zavala and a group of his loyal Mexican friends dismounting. Burnet pondered what could have happened. Lorenzo had started out way ahead of them. It did not take David long to reason why. As soon as he saw Lorenzo's face and looked into his hollow eyes, he could tell that the man was ill. He knew Lorenzo had been overly tired when he left after the convention to hide out from Santa Anna; and no doubt the exposure to drenching rains, with no protection out in the woods, had been more than his frail body could take.

It was hard to believe that this man, who had held every important government position in Mexico at one time or another, was now a fugitive; that his picture with a dead or alive sign beneath it was nailed upon saloon doors all over Texas — from the banks of the Rio Grande to the Redlands of the east.

David thought to himself, "How much greater the sacrifice of this man."

Others continued to stop in at the plantation during the day. One of these was a Negro boy named Joe; the president had summoned him to appear.

There was a certain aura about this boy that drew people to him like a magnet. He was the servant of the late William B. Travis and the only male survivor of the Alamo. Word spread that Joe was here and they jammed in all around him sitting and propping around the walls. Every neck was craned, every ear turned to hear what he had to say.

Joe stood rigid and looked uneasily at the strangers. He was a barefooted youth in a faded shirt of calico and homespun breeches that were extended by

25

long suspenders, but still gave evidence of being far too short for his storklike legs.

Compassion rose in Burnet as he looked into the Negro's face. He looked so scared and confused, like he wanted to run and had no place to go. His eyes were sad and old looking, like they had seen too much, too soon for his early years.

"Tell us what you remember about March 6 — your last day in the Alamo," Burnet asked him in a kindly voice. "Start from the beginning."

"Well," he stammered, standing on first one foot, then the other, "I remember first that loud, scary sounds woke us up, that it was dark — that I was cold.

"Mist'r Travis grabbed his gun and sword and shouted, 'Hurry, the Mexicans are coming!' Then I picked up my gun and followed him." His quivering lips parted slightly as though ready to speak but no words came out.

"Go on, boy," they insisted.

"They kept shootin' at us — and climbing the wall — two times we peeled 'em off." His voice was choked. "Then one got Mist'r Travis."

Burnet sat motionless and thickness climbed in his throat. "What did you do, Joe?"

The Negro rubbed his sleeve over his face to wipe away the tears. "I — ran — " he cried out hysterically. "I ran off and left Mist'r Travis."

By now he was crying uncontrollably from a heart that was broken. An awful hushed silence fell upon the men. Sympathy for the poor dejected boy swept through the crowd. Many a one remembered those letters from Travis and his pitiful pleas for help, and how only thirty-two brave souls from Gonzales had answered his call.

26

Each one could recall memories of their fallen friends and relatives that they would see no more. Sam Carson had learned how to duel from David Crockett back in Tennessee so he could avenge an enemy of his father. Now, his friend was gone — forever.

Burnet remembered how he was on his way to help Travis and had intended to stop over just long enough at the convention to get further help, when they talked him into staying.

Rob Potter had made a motion that they adjourn and go to Travis' aid; but Tom Rusk had opposed and helped beat down the motion, saying that we had to make a government first. Burnet looked at the secretary of war out of the corner of his eye and his face had turned ashen gray. Then he pondered over the outcome and wondered if they had gone whether things would have been any different — or any better, for Texas.

Later, Joe told the men more about the terrorizing day. He said that the third time the Mexicans tried to climb the walls, they made it over the top. A Mexican general passed by Travis and aimed a bayonet at him. Joe said that he thought his master was dead, but he wasn't, for he came up like a ghost rising from the dead and rammed a sword clear through the Mexican's body. Then both men fell and lay still in a pool of blood.

He went on to relate how they trampled over bodies, brown and white alike; of hearing the constant roar of cannons and crumbling walls; how Colonel Crockett, with his rifle "Old Betsy," and his men were found together with dead Mexicans all around them; that dying Jim Bowie shot from his cot as long as he had a breath of life in him.

27

Joe said when they found him hidden in one of the rooms that they shot at him, grazing his side. Just when a man was about to throw a bayonet at him, someone called a halt.

He went on to recall that the Mexicans stacked the bodies of our fallen heroes, layering them with wooden branches, and then drenched them with oil. As the torch was lighted and the flames began to leap sky high, he was led away. There were some more Negroes, a few Mexican women, and an Anglo-American woman with a baby that were with him. After questioning, they were all turned loose.

This Anglo-American woman with her child was Mrs. Susanna Dickinson, and Joe's story was very much the same one that she had told to Sam Houston upon reaching Gonzales.

How ironic that this final day of the battle was also on a Sunday. Little did they know that Fannin had surrendered that day and that this might turn out to be an even bloodier Sunday than the Alamo.

Monday: March 21, 1836

Jared Groce was up at the crack of dawn in the morning to greet his visitors as they came in for breakfast. This would be their last meal together, as most were leaving shortly for the capitol-to-be at Harrisburg.

The patriarch's manner put all in a reasonably happy mood, even Zavala, who had been feeling under the weather. With generous doses of quinine and a good night's rest, he had snapped back — giving evidence that he was ready for whatever the day held for him.

The little vice-president adjusted the fit of his coat about him with a flourish as he sat down. He looked up at his host with his snappy dark eyes and said in an eloquent manner, "My, with a meal like this, Señor Groce, we can travel far today."

The group agreed as they stuffed heartily on ham and eggs with all the trimmings. Burnet glanced across the table at Groce. He felt almost as if they had taken advantage of his goodness during these last three days.

But shortly after the last gulp of coffee, midst their showers of thanks for the fine meal and all that he had done for them, Groce sprang a surpriser. He approached the guests with a shrewd twinkle in his eyes, and said, casually but coldly, that he could use a little help; then he gave each one a bill, charging at the rate of three dollars per day, for food and lodging, which included both a man and his horse.

Burnet's head came round like he could not believe what he had heard and his mouth popped open. Some help — at three dollars a day? It was unheard of in these times not to be neighborly and share whatever one had, even if it was just a pallet or a piece of corn pone; besides most everyone else — many with much less wealth — was sending all the money they could rake and scrape together to support the army.

Why that old skinflint, the president thought. That ornery old penny pincher. But after a thunderstruck moment, he strummed through his mind some of the things Groce had done for them while they had been here. You couldn't quibble with the man over that. By actual rights they did owe him, though the price was a mite high. He supposed they should pay the bill, then forget about it.

He got the nods from the cabinet members (Bailey Hardeman was missing) and dug deep into his pocket. It was worse than pulling an abscessed tooth to part with this hard-to-come-by cash. He pulled out a roll of bills, sorted out the correct amount and said in a cool voice, "Here is your money, Mr. Groce."

Groce thanked them and accepted the money without batting an eyelash. The men tipped their hats and walked through the door into the fresh spring morning.

Burnet had just run through all the appropriate words he knew. And when he encountered the land and loaners outside ready to mount and follow along, he lowered the boom on them. He took a deep breath and spoke out what had been on his mind for several days. Then he ended up with, "Only the members of the cabinet and their appointed helpers will travel together today."

They could see Burnet meant every word he said. It was in his look and in the tone of his voice.

So the ruffled, lesser-lights flocked together like birds of a feather. "Some government," one of them was heard to remark, which pretty well summed up the raucous rumblings of the departing group.

Burnet wished later that he hadn't spouted off like that. But actually, it was good that he had issued this ultimatum. Aside from the fact that the new officers had a right to a certain degree of privacy, the road en route was too narrow to permit such a procession to keep abreast, it being little more than an oversized cow trail. Furthermore, food and lodging for such a large-sized group was out of the ques-

30

tion on this route where houses were of only modest size.

Despite the set-to to start off with, the day gave promise of a good one for the journey. The sun had burned away the fog that managed to tumble in from the Brazos River every morning. There was a gentle breeze to make things comfortable for them. It was what a farmer would say was a good day for "growing crops."

The government men cut stately figures as they reined their horses south, then east, toward Harrisburg. It took them through the fertile valley, across a prairie that gently sloped and dipped into graceful folds, and into grassy meadows dotted with bluebonnets, buttercups, and fiery little Indian blankets, intermingled with many others.

Each passing moment brought pleasing sounds as well as sights. Myriads of birds twittered and flittered amongst the trees along the fringe of the woodlands. But only Zavala made mention of their songs. He said it reminded him of the times when he was a boy in Yucatán and sat quietly listening, then dreaming great dreams of the future.

The rest of the group were more or less attuned to lend an eye or ear only for those that were suitable game such as the quail and dove, or a turkey's gobble and maybe the bark of a squirrel. There were plenty of these around, too, along with jackrabbits and cottontails.

However, the killdeer was one they all paid attention to. This handsome, cinnamon-topped bird with the white underparts was the settler's watch bird. If anybody dared to venture into their camp the killdeer never failed to warn them with its call of kill-dee, kill-dee.

The thirsty travelers were glad to happen upon a little creek. They stopped to water their horses and refresh themselves. Minnows darted in the sunlit splotches and tiny frogs hit the water with brief little splats.

Further evidences on the banks revealed this was a popular stop-off for others as well. There were raccoon tracks beside those of its fluffy-tailed cousin, the ringtail — both are heavy drinkers; hoofprints of the spotted fawn and its graceful mother, or antlered father, possums, skunks, coyotes — you name it, they had been there.

It was easy to understand why the Americans had taken such a liking to this beautiful new country. Land was free for the taking, there were no mountains to climb, no deserts to cross, and the Indians were fairly friendly. It held promises of great wealth and and much happiness.

But there was little to smile about now. It was like a blasted dream; as if you woke up one morning and puff, it was all gone, like the "wings of the wind." One did not have to look very hard to find clues to the effect that things were going badly.

Farmers had left their plows to fight for their rights. They had no idea when, or if, they would ever return. Acres and acres of fields lay bare. It was too bad. This had been a wet spring, which made for a good bottom season. There would have been bumper crops to harvest in the fall.

Ordinarily the cotton would be coming up at this time. And the corn should have been ready for thinning, its long narrow leaves rippling in the breeze like a shiny bright sea. This meant less money and a shortage of food for both man and beast, should the revolution last long.

Women and children had left their homes and joined others in the "Runaway Scrape," littering the landscape with lost and cherished possessions. As they advanced on the weary trek, they sorted out items to lighten their overloaded vehicles, stripping down only to bare essentials that were necessary to keep them alive. The winds had scattered the debris over the whole countryside.

David Burnet caught a glimpse of a tattered rag doll in the ditch beside him. It sent a chill through his bones — a little child's prized possession, gone. All because of one man who had set himself up as a dictator.

With so many away, the tired officials began to wonder if anyone was left for them to spend the night with. But they were fortunate to find Abram Roberts' household still intact.

A flyer arrived shortly afterwards reporting that Col. James Fannin had blown up the fort and left Goliad; you know, news traveled slow in those days. The officials were more conditioned by now to expect the worse and hope for the best.

They were also getting quite adept at letter writing. Tonight one was written to Treas. Bailey Hardeman, who had gone on ahead. It stated that things were taking shape and that they now had five thousand dollars in the treasury, which had been raised by donations.

However, it went on to say that the money was to be sent to Thomas F. McKinney of McKinney and Williams of Quintana, as part of a down payment for the forty thousand dollars' worth of supplies and ammunition that had been ordered for the army. An additional draft of ten thousand dollars on the bank at New Orleans had also been sent to the merchants.

The tired officials sacked out early. Sleep was much easier tonight. For the first time soldiers were camped around them, acting as guards for their protection.

Tuesday: March 22, 1836

The unofficial hanger-oners arrived at Abram Roberts' place in the morning just in time to join the presidential party. It was as if they had completely forgotten about the day before. You will recall that President Burnet had given the group a brush-off when they made ready to leave.

Burnet winced but did not say a word to them. He reckoned them to a bunch of red bugs — they got under his skin and itched but he supposed they were harmless.

The road forked here. They all took off leaving the Brazos River and headed southeast for Harrisburg, the new capital on Buffalo Bayou. If they were lucky, they would be there sometime after dark. But it would take a lot of long, hard riding — over forty miles worth.

It was just before noon when they reached Widow Burnett's house — not of the president's family. Since they knew of no other dwelling between there and Harrisburg, they stopped off there. The widow was still at home and didn't seem perturbed at all that Santa Anna was in Texas.

They dined sumptuously on hot roasted beef. There were stacks of thick yellow corn bread, which some crumbled into their tumblers and others dredged with fresh churned butter.

34

All free — for her country, she said, in an almost reverent tone. And she had a bunch of children to feed, too. It was a far cry from the attitude of their host back aways. She did charge a quarter though to feed each horse, saying that she was short of corn and would soon have to buy some; that she didn't know where the money was coming from, since her children were too small to work.

As the heads of state ventured farther along, the prairie land gave into timbers of yellow pine and oak trees. The sight of the tall stately trees and that red sandy soil quickened Burnet's pulse.

He braced his feet in the stirrups and stood up in his saddle as if to get a better view. It seemed like he had been away from his old stomping grounds for so long; actually it had been less than two weeks. So much had happened; so much water had run under the bridge.

He remembered the morning that he left. When the message from Travis came from the Alamo, the men of the municipality (similar to our county today) took action immediately. It was decided that some would go to the army and others would remain at home to take care of the women and children.

He had placed himself in the first group — to go. He said good-by to his family and then left for Washington-on-the-Brazos to find out the plans there.

Burnet had not been elected a delegate to go to the convention and this was somewhat of a blow but it never stopped him in the work of his country. Now, he was returning home as their first president of the Republic of Texas!

Zavala was elated, too. He was returning to a people who had confidence in him and believed in his cause for a democratic way of life. The famous exile had given a good account of himself and he took great pride in knowing he had gained the confidence of the convention delegates — enough to return as the first vice-president of the Republic of Texas!

But Zavala was not happy in the same way that Burnet was. So long as the revolution continued, he would work unceasingly for Texas! But once it ended and Santa Anna's centralist government was put down, he planned to return to Mexico as its president.

As its leader he would bring his poor oppressed people back to a democratic way of life. Originally he had had hopes of Texas rejoining Mexico as a free and independent state; then he would have been its president, too. But things had gone too far for that to ever happen.

Darkness overtook the horsebackers. The wind blew in from the gulf, bringing low gray clouds, which hung like a veil over the weary men. This hampered their way; there was no light of the twinkling star to guide them to their destination — only a pale sliver of a moon peeking around the clouds now and then.

Burnet knew the area like the palm of his hand and he led the way down the trail. Yapping coyotes and the call of a lonely wolf added to the eeriness. Screech owls were making weird sounds as if signaling for a death march. And there were panthers who might pounce out any moment. Too, each man knew full well that once they made a wrong turn and ever got into those vast cane brakes, they had had it.

It was well after dark by the time they reached Buffalo Bayou. Emotions of relief and thanksgiving surged through David Burnet as he approached its sandy banks and passed across the calm, placid waters. He sighted the hanging lanterns at the Harris house just beyond. It was as if they were waving a welcome to the weary men.

The house — one of the better dwellings in the village — had been built recently by Mrs. Jane Harris. She was a widow and had come from New York with her oldest son to take up where her late husband, John Richard Harris, had left off. To the side was a huge magnolia tree that stretched its giant flower-blossomed branches toward the dark and stately pines.

Mrs. Harris opened the doors wide to the stiff, tuckered-out travelers. And if she had possessed a red carpet she would have rolled it out for them. In her welcome, she told them she considered it a great honor for the new Republic to use her home as its capitol.

The officers were fortunate, indeed, to have such a generous and gracious hostess. She had not joined the runaways, but had stayed on; so she could extend them a special greeting and also make things more comfortable. Tired as they were, no polished gentleman — or unschooled one for that matter — could have kept from noticing that the widow was quite attractive.

And she was equally adept at handling any situation at hand. In no time at all, she had fed and bedded them down. For the heads of state — Burnet, Zavala, and Carson — there were beds, with pallets and make-downs for the rest.

It had been a long day. Being president wasn't easy, Burnet thought. He put his aching head upon the pillow and drifted off to sleep.

Wednesday: March 23, 1836

President Burnet plunged into his tasks this morning with gusto, tackling pressing problems that go with setting up a new capital. He was anxious to complete the preliminaries so he could ride home for a quick check on his family; they lived only a short distance away, across Buffalo Bayou on the north tip of Burnet's Bay.

The executive dashed off communiques, including one to Gen. Sam Houston, stating that two-thirds of the militia had been called up and that these men should be joining him shortly. The militia at that time was made up of citizens who protected their homes from the warlike Indians; it was similar to our National Guard today.

This was in answer to a request that the general had previously made asking the government to send him eight hundred men immediately. He was supposedly still waiting for the new recruits and supplies at Beason's on the Colorado River, near present-day Columbus.

Burnet was keeping a watchful eye on the weather. It showed signs of a storm in the making. The darkness of the sky to the north foretold the rapid approach of a wet Texas norther. He decided he must go now before it was too late.

He delegated the duties to the remaining officers, leaving Sam Carson in charge. Zavala was also going to his home nearby.

The two top officials were greeted with cheers as they rode from the capital on their high-stepping horses and through the village. There were some twenty dwellings, most of which were log cabins, that were strung out under the trees in helter-skelter

38

fashion. This was the empire of the Harris brothers, the most prominent of which was hostess Jane's late husband, John Richard.

The three New Yorkers gambled on the virgin forests at the junction of the two bayous — Buffalo and Brays — to make them rich, rather than the prairies. And it had paid off threefold.

Most noticeable, perhaps, was the general store, which was run by Jane's young son, Dewitt Clinton Harris. He sold everything in the alphabet from an axe to zinc buckets.

A group of idle rabble rousers were slouching on the steps of the store. They were whittling away and making a loud noise about the Mexicans in between chaws of tobacco. The likes of them irritated Burnet as he tipped his hat in passing. He was mighty tempted to pile off his horse and order the lazy scoundrels to go fight in the army where they could do some good. He had a feeling that it would come to that sooner or later.

The rising wind was shifting. It was carrying a pungent smell of burning sawdust from the steam sawmill. This was the first one of that kind in Texas and it provided jobs for most of the people here. It was hissing steam and slicing pines and oaks into planks, much of which would be loaded onto ships and sent to foreign ports.

There was no printing press, no newspaper, no school or church — not even a Roman Catholic chapel. A padre passed through here once in a while to administer the vows of the church to newcomers so they could legally hold property.

The chiefs of state took a sharp turn around the wind-rippled bend of Buffalo Bayou, which had all the marks of a good fishing spot. The stream was teeming with buffalo — a large edible fish of the sucker family. Incidentally, this was how the body of water came by its name, not from the four-footed beasts, as they did not choose to roam here.

As they rode farther away they passed several places that were being vacated by folks that were returning to the United States. These people were willing to sell their land for practically nothing, as they feared that the Mexicans would win. This was where Col. William Fairfax Gray had planned to make a few deals that day before going to Zavala's to visit.

Burnet supposed the reason Zavala had invited Gray, who was a land agent for some men in Washington, D.C., was that the two had bunked together during the convention. Burnet and the agent had been crossways with each other ever since they met there. He had to admit though the man did keep a fairly accurate account of the daily happenings.

The path eventually ended where Buffalo Bayou runs into San Jacinto Bay. This was where Zavala lived, in a small log house covered with planks. It was beautifully situated high on a knoll overlooking the water of the bays.

Burnet had a longer way to go and the storm was coming faster than he had expected it to. It was thundering and lightning all around, and the wind seemed to be increasing in force. It twisted the branches of the trees wildly about.

He noticed that the deer and mustang ponies were more kickey-up than usual and were skeltering off to shelter. According to old-timers, this was a sign of some sudden change in the weather. He knew he would have to hurry for there wasn't much time.

The lawmaker wanted more than anything else

40

at this moment to see his family, to find out if they were all right. Once that was done he would be ready to go back to the capital and tackle anything that might come up. He shrugged as he passed by the saw-mill. It had hurt to shut down and sell that mill. He wished he could have made a go of it like the Harrises did theirs. But he realized that he made a mistake in placing it in this location. And inexperienced help did not help matters any.

Then his face lit up with pleasure. He caught sight of his home, which was back from the bay a piece in the middle of an oak thicket. It was easy to understand why they had named the little plantation Oakland. It was scarcely bigger than an ordinary calf pasture (according to old settlers' standards) but it was home, and home is where the heart is.

The house was made of roughly hewn planks and was perched upon handmade bricks. Nearby was his fruit orchard, which he personally tended to with ever-loving care; he even had some orange trees. A few smaller houses were scattered out through the trees.

Hannah, would she be all right? And the little boys, Willie and Jacob? Would they all still be there?

William Este was around two and one-half and Jacob George was a tiny baby, who was a little over four months old. They had lost their oldest child, Sarah Mills, at birth.

But Burnet need not have worried. Just as he rode up and looked toward the house, Hannah came to the window. She parted the lacy curtains and peeked out, as if she had known all along that her David would be out there. Burnet's grim mouth slipped into a smile and happiness mounted in his eyes.

Meanwhile, back at Harrisburg, Sam Carson had penned a message to Col. James Morgan — the man

41

in charge of the port at Galveston — requesting that he come immediately to discuss security matters in regards to the capital and its bay area.

Carson had also sent a supply list to the commandant at Galveston for the following supplies: stationery, blankets, washbowls, plates, cups and saucers, tumblers, loaf sugar, tea, corn, flour, and liquors suitable for genteel men to drink.[2]

And Tom Rusk busied himself with messages to other imminent people asking that they also come for consultation on the pressing problems. One of these was to John R. Jones, the postmaster general of a former government that had collapsed.

Thursday: March 24, 1836

It was cold and dreary out this morning. Heavy rains had pelted down during the night, flooding the countryside. A gusty northeast wind shook the David Burnet house and tree branches beat against its rooftop. Old-timers dubbed the disturbance as the proverbial "Easter Spell."

The president and the first family were huddled around the fireplace. Burnet had the children in his lap, his strong arms wrapped around them. For the moment a sense of tranquility settled over him as he watched the crackling flames. The warmth and affection for his loved ones smothered out his gloomy thoughts. In their presence he felt an optimism that lifted him out of the depths of despair.

---

2 Andrew F. Muir, "The Municipality of Harrisburg, 1835-1836," *Southwestern Quarterly*, vol. LVI, July 1952, p. 45.

He hesitated to break the beautiful moment. But then he made a mental note of the steps he had taken for their safety and evacuation, in event it came to that, charging his most obedient servant to see that they were carried out. Yes, he had accomplished his mission.

He glanced over to Hannah. The sparkling flames reflected in her starry eyes. She shifted toward him and flashed him a knowing smile.

"I have to go now," he said, in a slow deliberate manner.

Her face went plaster white. "Oh, no, David," she said, cupping her hand over her mouth.

The president could not keep from noticing the sad look upon her face. He put the little ones down ever so gently, then pulled his dearly beloved wife toward him. As he tightened his arms around her, he felt her body trembling.

"I understand," she said, in a slow, soft voice.

"I'll have to leave the seat of the saddle, today," he said, in as light a tone as he could muster, "and take to the paddle."

"So much rowing," she whispered, "all the way to Harrisburg."

"Oh, Zavala is just a stone's throw across the bay," he assured her. "I'll make it there before noon. Then we can go together and take turns with the oars."

Hannah Burnet lifted her head back and squared her frail shoulders in typical pioneer fashion. She never seemed so beautiful as at that moment, trembling with grief but yet managing a heroic smile. "I know — you must go."

They both nodded. With a quick military stride he walked out the door into the wind. It seemed to be blowing in every direction, pushing more rain clouds to the front. He sloshed toward the boat ramp, picking the high spots to step on along the way.

As the president shoved the boat into the water, he turned his eyes toward shore and waved a fond farewell. The small boat, hardly bigger than a canoe, bobbled up and down in the choppy waters. Flocks of gulls were flying overhead, crying out a sad farewell for the departing executive, as he paddled across the bay.

Then he turned and looked back across the turbulent waters from which he came, trying hard to catch a glimpse of his beloved three, though he knew full well he would not be able to see them that far away. Somehow, he had the feeling that Hannah, too, was scanning the bay in search for him. "This is what we fight and work for," he thought as he pulled more swiftly upon the oars toward the other side.

Zavala was there to greet his chief with a pertly strut. "Good morning, Señor Burnet," he called out in a throaty voice. "How are you?"

"Well, Lorenzo, after all this rowing, I'm a bit spent."

"Well, come on to the house. Emily has a meal ready and that should be just what you need."

"I'm ready; you don't have to twist my arm one bit."

"Let's go," Zavala said, helping Burnet ashore.

Emily Zavala, a young, black-eyed beauty from New York, had taken time out to prepare a tasty meal in between caring for her three young children and helping her stepson (Lorenzo, Jr.) make ready for the army. There was a French influence in the decor of the little home, due to the fact, perhaps, that

Zavala was minister in that country before coming here.

After the meal, the two executives returned to the beach and took their places in the center of the boat. Zavala made ready to man the boat first. He slipped an oar into the lock and there was a sharp click; then he sent the craft through the murky waters with sure, even strokes, easing it toward Buffalo Bayou.

Burnet's thoughts drifted to those unsettled problems that would rise up to meet him within a short time. Soon the two were discussing what to do about them when they returned. The one that seemed to plague the men the most was the land-loan deal. Still there were others, such as how to get Houston to fight, the whereabouts of Santa Anna, the condition of Fannin and his troops, and any number of things.

By midafternoon they brought the boat through to drag on the stones of the beach at Harrisburg. They learned that Sam Carson had taken great strides toward setting up things satisfactorily.

Friday: March 25, 1836

The first thing on the agenda this morning was the loan. It could not be tabled much longer.

They agreed on satisfactory terms as to how the contract should be drawn up. If nothing else happened it would be ready for the signing the following day. The moneylenders felt that at least they had made some headway and they were quite elated over it.

Then Burnet read a message from Colonel Morgan, which said, "The inhabitants [on the Trinity] & around the Bay, on the east side, are so alarm'd — so panic struck that they are flying in every direction — Those who can't get away by land are pushing off in *boats* — Most of the horses there are in great demand and I fear we shall find difficulty in obtaining what will be requisite for the use of the Govt. . . . The *Negroes* high upon the Trinity have manifested a disposition to become troublesome & and in some instances *daring* — They had endeavored to enlist the *Coshatti Indians* on their side & come down & murder the inhabitants and join the Mexicans. . . ."[3]

It all ran together — black slaves, redskins, and brown, masterminding Mexicans — making a horrendous picture before Burnet's eyes: white women and children being scalped or burned alive in their flaming homes; another wild flight of escape even more terrifying than the last one.

It was as if one huge diamondback rattlesnake were slithering and rearing its ugly, tricornered head while it flicked a forked tongue. The dry buzzing of its rattles had already begun. Soon it would wind its rough, scaly body into a symmetrical coil tighter around the Texans. Then it would spring and strike with its venom-filled fangs — and Texas would be no more.

Volunteers from within the Republic as well as from the United States were not coming in fast enough to meet the oncoming crisis. Something more drastic had to be done to step up the war effort.

Burnet, with the help of the cabinet, did some serious thinking and collaborating. They made up their minds to declare the country under martial law.

---

3 Chambless, Beauford, *The Ad Interim Government of the Republic of Texas*, Rice Institute, Houston, Texas, June 1949, pp. 23-24.

If Texas was going to gain her independence *all* would have to pay the price.

The entire Republic was divided into military districts. Committees of public safety were given the go-ahead to confiscate anything necessary for the good of the army. Every man was ordered to report to the draft board posthaste. With this went a strong warning for those who defected.

All of Harrisburg was in a wild frenzy!

Saturday: March 26, 1836

David Thomas had slept little the night before. This morning he was up long before dawn. He read the loan contract, with which all had been in agreement the day before — taking it line by line. Being the attorney general, he was charged with the duty of giving legal advice concerning this loan — and it was to be made official that day by signatures of the cabinet.

He was growing more concerned by the minute about the section on control of money and land for business profits at public expense. He paced nervously back and forth. He confronted each fellow officer about that part as they entered and started making preparations for the meeting.

The loan men gathered to await the belated signing. They seemed uncommonly solemn, as if they rather half-suspected that something amiss was in the air.

If so, their feelings were justified. For doubting Thomas leaned to place the ill-fated paper upon the table. Then he rose to his full height, gaining in

47

stature as well as stamina. His peers knew that he was up to speak his mind about the whole thing. His doubts were cast aside.

"Gentlemen," he said with an icy stare, "I feel duty bound to express my feelings on this matter before we get on with the signing." He cited the instances that most concerned him. He went to great lengths of explanation and wound up recommending that it again be tabled for future negotiation.

A rising tide of resistance marked the manners of the money men. They rebuked the attorney general and made a pitch about their fear of how things were going from bad to worse, that something drastic had to be done now.

To argue with this attorney general — whose steel-like determination had advanced him up to the ranks of captain in the United States Independent Volunteers Cavalry Company within a few short months, then on as a delegate to the convention, and now to his present position — was like pouring water on a duck's back.

Burnet, who was of a somewhat procrastinating nature anyhow, agreed with the rest of the five cabinet members (Hardeman still not there) to postpone the signing. Though peace still prevailed within the official family, a hornet's nest had been stirred up among the outsiders.

It was at this time unnoticed in the frenzy of madness, that a new arrival rode up. He hitched his horse and stepped upon the porch. Then someone noticed for the first time that he was trying to make himself heard.

The mob curbed their anger and ringed about the man to hear what he had to say. The messenger poured jumbled bits of information about Goliad.

48

He told how he went there to help; that Fannin had been boxed in by the Mexican Gen. José Urrea; that it was impossible to get through their lines; and he feared that the odds were against the Texans.

The cabinet members, due to such slow lines of official communication, knew nothing about this. They were also in the dark about Houston's plans. They were unaware that the Mexican forces, under Gen. Joaquin Ramirez y Sesma, had caught up with Houston and were setting up on the opposite bank (west side) of the Colorado River.

No artillery had yet arrived to help Houston and only a thin trickle of supplies from Galveston had reached him. Men were coming into camp in singles, or small groups, seldom more than that.

It was clear that the Mexicans had him at their mercy and could overtake and annihilate him at will. He laid the blame on Burnet and his cohorts. He started running again.

Despite Houston's misgivings about the horse-back officers, they were making desperate attempts to fill his needs. It was decided that Rob Potter must go immediately to check on the ports and lay out further fortifications, so they could keep their supply lines open.

Potter, the swashbuckling daredevil of the sea who had challenged the navies of the world, welcomed a chance to battle it out with the Mexican commanders. He had been as restless as the unrelenting wind for the last few days; but now his black eyes were shining with excitement.

"The fate of the nation might well be in your hands, Rob," said Burnet. "Especially if we can't get Sam Houston to stand up and start fighting."

"I'm ready for anything, boss," said Potter, who didn't especially go for Sam Houston either.

Then he swaggered out into the wind that was blowing unceasingly inland from the gulf, whistling as if it was giving out a warning that all was not well out where he was going. But knowing that Burnet and the rest had confidence in him, he hastened on down the way.

The bleak island of Galveston (though it was one of the best locations in the Gulf of Mexico) and the four, secondhand ships of the Texas navy might well have been the last hope of defense for Texas, true. But what could be done by the secretary with such little schooners — a ship with two or more masts — which were manned for the most part by would-be sailors?

There was the *Liberty*, which carried four to six guns. It had been a privateer and was used by its captain to seek fame and fortune. A group of only twenty to fifty men sailed on this smallest of their small vessels.

The *Invincible*, built in a shipyard at Baltimore, Maryland, for African slave trade, was the fastest ship they had; it was also the heaviest in her ordinance. Seventy men kept it afloat and manned its eight guns, which were of varying sizes. The two eighteen-pounders were the deadliest and longest-range weapons the fledgling fleet had to offer.

The eight-gun *Brutus*, which carried forty men, was also fitted out as a privateer originally by the Allen brothers (men who later founded the city of Houston). It had to lay in dry dock at New Orleans for some time for extensive repair work; too, there were some legal aspects that had to be cleared before it was ready to be commissioned for the Texas navy.

50

Due to all this delay, it was the last one to be purchased.

The seven-gun *Independence,* with a crew of forty men, was the flagship of the newborn navy. The vessel had been a United States revenue cutter prior to its sale at New Orleans. It was already roaming along the coast and ready to attack an enemy with the fierceness of a lioness defending her cubs against the onslaught of a half-starved wolf.

Sunday: March 27, 1836

Sam Carson sat at the long table with his four fellow workers; you remember that Potter left the day before and that Hardeman was still at his home. Carson was bent over barely picking at the bountious breakfast, which Jane Harris had spread before them on this Palm Sunday. He made no attempt to enter into the conversation of the group, as if he was up-tight about something.

Ordinarily the secretary of state would be talking out in his silver-toned voice in much the same way that he gave out with hymn singing at camp meetings in North Carolina.

Burnet, who sat beside him, noticed this and sensed a certain tension which was not normal for the jolly young man. Perhaps, the president reasoned, he was suffering a recurrence of that chronic ailment of his. Carson had come to Texas seeking a more suitable climate for his health as well as to mend his fortune. His friends in Congress — Davy Crockett,

Rob Potter, and Sam Houston — had convinced him he would find both here.

"You feel all right?" Burnet asked him.

Carson lifted his head and smiled, then nodded as if to say he was OK. He was still handsome in spite of his sickness, which had left him with a deeply lined face. He looked at them with sunken eyes, then he took a shallow breath before parting his lips to form words that they seemed eager to hear.

"Men, are we going to keep faith with the people of Texas?" he asked.

"Why, yes," they agreed, as if to say they thought that was understood.

"Well, it looks to me the way we are headed, we're fighting a losing battle. If Santa Anna doesn't take us, the land men will. Those terms — they're just too unequal."

Carson placed a written account upon the table stating what he thought of the loan problem. At this time he made some off-the-cuff statements, which had some of the same underlying tones of what Thomas had said the day before. All this slick talking had about convinced him that these men were out to strip Texas naked of its prize virgin lands. He felt it was their bounden duty to help guard this important earthly resource.

His listeners hung on to every word, some nodding their approval. It was easy to see that doubt was growing steadily within the cabinet. The previous day it was Thomas, today it was Carson. Who knew which one it would be the next day.

Zavala, who was ailing again, broke the silence by getting up from the table. He trudged to the window and looked out. He was expecting Lorenzo, Jr. any minute to stop by on his way to report to General

Houston. It was the young man's first time for battle. Would it also be his last one?

Unknown to these men — a handful of Texans in the quiet little town of Goliad had been hearing sounds of continuous shots since daybreak. Their faces were full of fear and they were in a state of shock — they were scarcely able to take in all that was happening there.

Col. James Walker Fannin and his brave young volunteers had been cut down in cold blood by Gen. José Urrea's firing squad, as ordered by Santa Anna. Over three hundred dead soldiers were sprawled on the chalky hillside, which was growing red from blood spurting out of the bullet holes of their shredded bodies.

Santa Anna, the super sleuth of slaughter, had wracked the Texas army. Remember the tragedy of the Alamo a few Sundays before? This time it was Goliad, which was less than a hundred miles down on the same San Antonio River and same day of the week. Sunday, bloody Palm Sunday!

Monday: March 28, 1836

Threatening clouds darkened the sky and cast an early gloom upon the men at the head of the Horseback Government. Their weariness was in keeping with the thin mist that seemed to grow thicker as the day wore on.

Guards sloshed in with five young Mexicans that had been arrested for spying two days before. Since Zavala was the one most fluent in the Spanish language, it was understandable why the rest of the men leaned upon him to take the lead during the trial.

The ailing vice-president coughed until he cleared his throat, then spat in the brass spittoon and began to question the suspects. During the investigation one proved to be a loyal Texan and was released with apologies.

The other four were proven guilty. They were sentenced to work on building bunkers for gun implacements overlooking the entrance to Galveston Bay. A guard was assigned to accompany them and they took off.

There was a heavy silence in the executive mansion. Each cabinet member was busy with his own thoughts and feelings about the prisoners. Only the sound of raindrops that had begun to fall upon the rooftop broke the stillness.

It was Zavala who broke the long silence. "Such young boys," he said, "like my Lorenzo. This is no fault of theirs — I hope they find shelter tonight in some empty house."

"Or under an arbor," put in Carson, whose face was as gray as the leaden sky.

They heard the squish of hoofs cutting through the mud; then the sound of footsteps approaching the door — followed by a sharp, quick knock. A gleam of hope flashed into their eyes as they momentarily stared at each other. Oh, lawdy, could it be news of Sam Houston?

It had been some time since they had heard from him — officially that is. Tom Rusk was especially concerned about his whiskey-drinking buddy. No ifs and buts about it, young Rusk still thought Houston was the greatest.

But David Burnet, who never drank anything

54

stronger than buttermilk, felt differently about the general and his "lifting of the jug." There was a slow-burning resentment welling up inside over the way Houston had ignored him and kept him in the dark about his plans as well as his whereabouts. After all he, Burnet, was the head of this Republic, not that cowardly drunkard.

The caller was Edward Gritten, their translator, who worked in the print shop of the *Telegraph and Texas Register* at San Felipe. They gathered around him as he peeled off his drippy coat and hat, anxiously awaiting news from the general — so they thought.

But it turned out that he had not even the faintest knowledge of Houston's whereabouts. Instead he proceeded to give out with the latest on Col. Juan Almonte's recent arrival in Santa Anna's camp.

"Oh," they said, unsuccessfully trying to conceal the disappointment on their downcast faces. It was as if the low-lying clouds were a curtain that had come down and shut them off from the rest of the world.

Thomas was the one to lash out. "All this snooping and spying and groping for news but never quite getting the right thing at the right time. This is more disgusting than dealing with those sneaky land men."

While this was going on at Harrisburg, Sam Houston and his disorderly mob were zigzagging across the country, through boggy, snake-infested briar and bramble patches, in a desperate effort to throw the Mexicans off their tracks. Fortunately, they made it to San Felipe on the Brazos River and put up for the night. The tired and wily old general would not be sending out any communiques that night, either.

Tuesday: March 29, 1836

It was a beautiful spring day. Only a few high clouds were floating in the azure blue sky. Growing plants, beside the shimmering waters of Buffalo Bayou, had taken on a fresh new look in various shades of green. Buds on the magnolias were grasping for the bright warm sun and giving promise of creamy white blossoms.

The air was scented with the poignant odor of moist pine needles. It was such a fresh, clean, and invigorating smell — one that made you breathe deep to take in all the air that your lungs can hold.

A steamboat was coming into sight around the bend. It was the *Cayuga*, returning to its home base in Harrisburg. Her captain, William Plunkett Harris, had christened her with this name for his hometown in faraway New York. Harris, by the way, was hostess Jane Harris' brother-in-law.

The sound of the steamer's shrill whistle was one that the villagers recognized. It was as welcome as the fresh breath of spring to them. For not only would it be bringing in the much-needed and eagerly awaited-for supplies, but also passengers who could and would give out with exciting bits of news from the outside world.

They harkened to its signal and began to walk down in small groups to watch the squat little steamer sweep up the bayou toward its landing. Choppy waves could be seen slapping against its sides as the paddles made their slow burdensome turns.

Watching it pull alongside the dock, they almost

forgot that a war was waging, that Fannin and his men had not yet been accounted for, that Houston — according to a recent arrival who had galloped in from his camp — was high-tailing it off again up the Brazos Valley, that his men were deserting, and that Santa Anna was hot on their heels.

Bailey Hardeman was standing with Burnet, Carson, Rusk, and Thomas; Zavala was too sick to leave his bed. Hardeman arrived somewhat earlier in the day.

He had already been briefed on the loan negotiations. It didn't take long for the wily, ex-cannoneer, who had fought under Andrew Jackson as a lad of seventeen, to find out that this issue was as hot as the lead he had fired out of his cannon down in those swamps of New Orleans.

But for the moment they, too, seemed to forget the issue and entered into the welcoming. New arrivals stepped upon the banks and huge bulky cargo came tumbling in behind them.

That is, all except Burnet. He shifted on first one foot and then the other. He had a faraway look, as if he was unaware of what was going on around him.

He had just finished work on a proclamation, one that was stronger than any that he had ever issued before. In this one it stated to some effect that any man who left Texas during this trying time or refused to fight, or gave aid to the enemy, would lose his citizenship and give up hold of any lands he might claim in the Republic.

He went over those sentences word for word in his mind, searching to see if he had covered all that was necessary. Then all of a sudden a look of pained surprise crossed over his face and his mouth flew

open momentarily. He had forgotten something —
the officers.

Quickly, he turned and started back toward the
house, side-stepping puddles from the preceding day's
rain. He was completely oblivious to the happy get-
together of friends and fellow passengers down upon
the sandy shore. He knew what he had to do, like
it or not.

The president detested Houston and thought it
was shameful that he was retreating. But now he
must lay aside all personal feelings. They were both
caught up in this storm of destruction. Together they
must arise to meet the enemy. Together they must
strengthen the army for the onslaught.

He walked across the porch and on down the hall
to his stuffy little room, leaving the door open to
let in the soft, gentle breeze. Without further ado he
went to his desk. With pen in hand he drafted a
further demand that all commissioned officers were
to report and/or return to Houston within ten days
or their commissions would be revoked.

When the sun began to dim, darkness, like weariness, hovered over the president. And yet he still had
another executive session to attend that day. Something had to be done about Houston.

Presently in San Felipe, huge flames of fire were
leaping toward the sky. Houston had left the town
burning to the ground.

Wednesday: March 30, 1836

The word was out about Houston running again,

that he was headed north up the valley of the Brazos River. The little capital at Harrisburg was overrun with people. It had caused a strange excitement to swoop over them, like the hot sultry air that hovered over the village.

They were gathering and talking loudly in the streets. They were scared and didn't know where to turn — like frightened cattle who want to stampede but don't know which direction to go. They kept shouting back and forth, "What does the general mean?"

"What the hell is going to happen to us?" one broke in, still a little drunk from the night before.

"Yeah," sounded off another. He was one of those who had just left Houston, supposedly to check on the families. But judging from looks and actions, he was a war slacker; it was doubtful that the general would ever see the likes of him again.

"Maybe it's a good thing we haven't come to final terms on that loan," remarked one of the surly money men with contempt in his voice.

"What's an army for, anyway?" shouted someone else.

Within the walls of the executive mansion, the officers of the Republic were asking the same questions — plus many others. Would this ruin the chances of getting help from the United States? What effect would it have on our credit? How about the loan? Yes, and how can we stop another panic?

While these weighty questions were being tossed back and forth, Lorenzo de Zavala lay ill a few doors down. He was suffering a recurrence of chills and fever. Lorenzo, Jr., who had delayed his ride to join Houston as a volunteer in the cavalry unit, was at his father's bedside. The doctor was checking him over.

After a lengthy deliberation it was decided that the ailing vice-president should return to his home for more intensive care and rest.

The handsome young cavalier led his father through the frustrated mob toward the boat landing. In passing, his sharp black eyes couldn't help but notice some of their suspicious-looking stares. A smattering of words that were both boastful and profane were scattered throughout the throng. Snide remarks were audible about spics and spies and greasy geezers.

All of a sudden a big, ugly-looking brute shouted out, "We ought to string up every damned Mesikan in Texas." Then he pointed a grimy finger toward the Zavalas. "Including them two yellow-hided s—."

There were just enough agitators in the crowd to urge him on. With their encouragement he started closing in on the pair. Angry resentment and hatred against all Mexicans — friend and foe alike — was building up to a fever pitch. Racial prejudice had reared its ugly head.

The bantam, hot-blooded young Mexican stopped short. He had a quick temper by nature and the first natural impulse was to snap back. It showed in his face and eyes, as he knotted his fists and met the big man's glary gaze.

Sensing this, the father tugged at his arm just in time to stop the fight. The eyes of father and son met and held. Then they exchanged a few words in Spanish.

The youth hesitated for a few moments, then gave a nod. His quick temper had cooled down and a smile softened the lines around his tight-set mouth. There was an understanding between the two. Both knew there was too much at stake right now to stir up further trouble.

60

He slipped his arm around his father for support and they continued their slow advance, paying no heed to the hecklers. As he put his father safely into the boat, he bade him a fond adiós and watched the thin, stooped figure as far as his sad eyes could see — until it slipped around the bend toward their home a short distance away.

He turned toward the hitching rack, where his horse was saddled up ready to go. A few other raw recruits were waiting to go with him.

Tom Rusk was supposed to have taken to that trail today, also; it had been decided that the secretary of war was the one to straighten Houston out, even take away his command if need be.

But Rusk had had quite a night and was unable to make it that day. His grayish pallor showed under the wiry stubble of a two days' growth of whiskers and his eyes were bleary as he squinted into the blazing sun to watch the horsebackers mount up.

Young Lorenzo swung into the saddle. Though slight in stature, he rode tall and straight through the town and over the bayou into the narrow trail where danger lay at every turn. He was well aware of the odds that he would never make it. If a Texan or the bow-and-arrow boys didn't pick him off for an enemy, chances are Santa Anna would, for he would now probably have to cross the Mexican line before he could get to Houston. The one thing in his favor was that he was not entirely alone.

However, the danger of the heavy odds seemed only to add to his zest for the hazardous game of revolution. "I, too, am a loyal Texan," the brown-skinned young man said to his fellow Anglo horsebackers. "And I'll fight for her till they shoot me out of the saddle."

61

Thursday: March 31, 1836

With Rusk packed up for his trip to General Houston's headquarters and Carson laying plans to leave also (because of his health), today had to be the showdown for settling the loan problem. And they finally did come to some final terms to which all could affix their signatures.

Burnet, the grizzled old veteran of revolutions, looked with a puzzled face at Rusk, who was going over the briefings that were to go to Houston. Would the young secretary of war carry out their orders in the final analysis?

Burnet — along with the other members, including Rusk — had gone along with the general when he pulled out of Gonzales on the Guadalupe River, even though they felt it caused the "Runaway Scrape"; they questioned his retreat from the Colorado River and failure to hold the line; but this was the last straw.

Now was the time to show some grit. All of the Texas frontier lay open to the sickening savagery of massacre and torture. Would Rusk have the courage to stand up to him and kick him out, if necessary? Or would he just fall in with Houston and run along with him?

For the fraction of a moment the older man doubted. Then he realized that the young protégé of the illustrious John C. Calhoun in the United States was into this as deep as the rest. Hadn't he given up a successful law practice without batting an eyelash? And wasn't he the one who had said to some effect during the final hours of the convention that he thought we were in one hell of a fix — that to get out of it we'd have to fight like the devil?

If he was a judge of men, as he believed himself to be, Rusk was a square shooter and a loyal Texan, a gunfighter and law-and-order man with steel in his backbone. Yes, he was a man that could and would rule with the rod of iron, unbending.

And almost as Rusk folded the message and put it in his pocket, Houston was also pressing a communique. Believe it or not, he in turn was at odds with the government for leaving Groce's and running out on him to Harrisburg; and he planned to keep on reminding them about how they had kept him in the dark during their days in the saddle. He was then camped at Groce's Landing on the west side of the Brazos River, within a stone's throw of the steamboat *Yellow Stone* also across from where the Horseback Government was a while back. Remember "The Retreat"?

Friday: April 1, 1836

Tom Rusk was the man of the hour. Today he must go to Houston and try to save Texas. It was up to him to make the right decisions at the right moment. He had only to make one wrong move and all would come tumbling down like a set of stacked dominoes.

It isn't hard to imagine how the young man felt when he accepted the challenge to fight for his country. Heavy odds were against him and he might well end up strumming a harp.

63

But the hard-riding, straight-shooting Rusk was ready to go into the field of battle. He mounted his horse with a quick twisting movement. His jaw was set firmly as he adjusted his pistols in the holster against his lean, hard-muscled thighs — within easy reach of his fast-moving hands.

"So long, partners," he said, as he nudged his horse and rode off with his following. "See you later."

After the send-off, Burnet was the first to break the tense moment. He murmured to Carson, "Well, Sam — you're next."

"Perhaps it would have been better if I had gone with them," he replied, as he watched the horsebackers disappear into the wilderness.

Carson's once melodious voice was now toneless and one could detect a sorrowful note. He was to go to Washington, D.C. for further help (he had asked for this) as soon as he recuperated at the family plantation up in Red River country.

"I know, Sam," answered Burnet, in an understanding voice like a father who tries to console a troubled son. "But you're too stove up."

He was appalled at Carson's run-down condition. He looked like a shaky old man on his last jag. Such a sad expression covered his thin, flushed face. He had every symptom of typhoid fever.

The understanding president placed his hand upon the secretary's bony, stooped shoulders. "Once you get on the mend, you can be of more help to us back in the East," he said. "Just don't stay too long — we need you back here, too."

Carson nodded and showed a thin smile.

Burnet twisted his head to one side and spotted Thomas and Hardeman nearby. Thank goodness, they would still be here to help him carry on during the trying days ahead. All he said to them was, "We must pull closer together — and tighten up our commitments."

Meantime, rumors were that the Mexican army was within practically a stone's throw of what was left of San Felipe after the burning; and Houston was still a few miles farther up from there.

Saturday: April 2, 1836

The *Cayuga* was shoving off down Buffalo Bayou. It was loaded to the hilt with passengers leaving Texas. Ailing Sam Carson was one of the many on board the squat little steamer.

David Burnet outdid himself to be cheerful as he joined in with the farewells that go with a departing boat. It was hard to bottle up his sad emotions. Somehow he had a strange feeling that it would be a long time before they met again.

After a while he turned toward the scattering people that were around him. There were such quizzical looks upon their sad faces — as if to say, why don't you do something, Burnet?

Yes, he was all they had to turn to, like the runaways that were camped out on Lynch's Prairie (across from Zavala's place). They were also expecting him to deliver them out of the jaws of the enemy.

Up until now they had been fairly safe — uncomfortable and scared, but safe. It wasn't like that anymore. He had to get those women and children out of there — before it was too late.

Each passing moment was harder than the last.

Only two were left to help him shoulder the responsibilities. Oh, if Zavala could only come back.

Sunday: April 3 — Saturday: April 9, 1836

It was Easter — a time when many of us today think of songs and flowers and ringing church bells to call us together for the joyful celebration of "His Glorious Ascendency."

David Burnet awoke to a beautiful sunshiny Sunday. He wanted to be alone for a while — to meditate and to think things through.

But his trend of thought was broken abruptly by the belated news that Goliad had fallen the week before on Palm Sunday. A few escapees were staggering into the capital with their horrible stories of death and disaster. For a long moment Burnet looked stunned. First the Alamo — and now Goliad.

With Fannin, as well as King and Ward upon his mind, he naturally feared the worst from Santa Anna. His mighty army was marching this way. There was no doubt in his mind as to who would be the next target — the heads of state, with Zavala going first.

As far as his eyes could squint in the bright sun he could see people running and scattering over the bayou like a covey of quail at the sound of a hunter's gun — some falling from exhaustion. They were bound for the ferry down at Lynch's, which was the only way they had of crossing over.

Zavala (thank goodness he was back after a narrow escape from a sniper on his way up) reported that hordes of people were still waiting at the ferry; the dreaded disease of cholera was sweeping through their

66

camps; and malaria, caused by mosquitoes — which were at the peak of their peskiness — was also taking a heavy toll on the half-starved victims.

The president and his three colleagues listened to complaints that were coming in ninety to nothing about the ferry keeper. They said that he was too slow in shuttling back and forth, his fees were outlandishly high, and that he overloaded his ferry and herded them in like cattle. Many were attempting to cross on makeshift rafts or logs and trees; others even dared to swim across — often drowning in the process.

Burnet assigned guards to try to straighten out the keeper. His eyes were hard, his voice low-pitched, as he demanded that all boats — sailboats, rowboats, ferryboats, any kind of conveyance that would float — be pressed into service to put the people safely over on the other side and away from the Mexican army.

But his voice cut as he lashed out at those "lazy hounds" of the village who refused to chop wood for the steamer so it could take passengers down to Galveston.

They still put him off until the very last — just went on whittling and spitting tobacco juice, all the while cussing Houston or the government. Lucky for those scoundrels that someone got off with the president's pistols. He was so irked, there might have been even fewer left.

All that day and far into the night Burnet labored in his office, seeking to allay panic by issuing reassuring proclamations. He proclaimed to the citizens as a whole, imploring them to the army and warning that all would be lost unless they came forth. He even offered a captain's rank to any man who would bring in fifty-six volunteers, a major's rank for three hundred volunteers, a colonel's rank for five hundred

67

volunteers, and a brigadier general's rank for one thousand volunteers. But it did little good.

There was a white moon that shed its ghostly light over the almost-deserted capital. Through the window Burnet sighted shadowy figures still trudging onward. There was the whimpering of a dog off in the distance. Perhaps it was some family pet that had been lost or left behind in the shuffle. Sooner or later, the officers would have to go, too. But not now.

His white hair was rumpled, his face sweat streaked. His nerves were pulled tautly. He was hungry and sleepy and utterly weary in every bone and muscle on this Easter day.

The president continued all the rest of the week desperately trying to calm the fugitives and strengthen the army. A special proclamation went out to the citizens of the Brazos; one to the Redlanders in the east; another to the Nacogdoches safety chairman, urging him to make a record of all draft evaders who crossed into the United States and to take away their guns and horses.

His stiff fingers were stained with ink. He had trimmed his feathered pens until they were down to the end of their tips. Everything was blurred, just like in the nightmares that had ripped through his sleep for so many nights. His eyes were bloodshot from lack of rest. Fear clamped his heart in an icy grip.

It was a greatly worn Burnet when he received a message from Sam Houston toward the end of the week, telling the president in so many words that he should keep his nose out of the army's business.

This rankled Burnet beyond endurance. He went into a rage that rose to a fever heat. His face turned crimson as a pepper bush that was flaming with red hot chili pods.

68

"Of all the — !" he burst out.

Burnet was so worked up that he did not notice he was talking out loud as he wrote the following letter:

> Sir: the enemy are laughing you to scorn. You must fight them. You must retreat no farther. The country expects you to fight. The salvation of the country depends on your doing so.[3]

Burnet was all washed out after this and he felt weak and limber as a wet dishrag. But he was relieved in a sense to get it out of his system.

His thoughts turned to events of the past few days with a feeling of defeat. True, a few volunteers were trickling in from the states. The people were as rational as could be expected under these perilous times. Most had been evacuated safely. But he had been unable to muster but a few supplies. He did not know where to turn. Where was all the help that those so-called friends from the United States were going to send?

Robert Potter was in Galveston Bay trying to get some supplies through. He was also rounding up the people that were left in that area to take them to safety. He was not averse to rescuing the pretty women, either — especially during wartimes. It was during one of his onshore and back-in-the-saddle days that he met Mrs. Harriet Page — every young man's dream of "Mrs. America."

He spotted the beautiful woman walking in his direction along a muddy trail. When their eyes met,

---

[3] Barker, E. C., "The San Jacinto Campaign," *Quarterly of Texas State Historical Association,* IV, p. 330.

he stopped his horse; and before she could object, he had her up on his horse in nothing flat. "I can carry double," he told her in a very convincing tone.

The horse gave a jolt and Harriet grabbed hold of her liberator and tightened her arms around his waist so she would not fall. This bounce marked the beginning of the wildest, most talked-about love affair of the century. Potter said that he took this lithe and lovely creature to the *Flash* to save her — which no one believed wholeheartedly then, or now.

Potter's handsome appearance captivated many other pretty damsels in distress. And he brought more than a few of them to this armed schooner for protection. Never did a secretary of the navy ever have a more charming crew — the decks any shinier — and food more tastefully served.

This privateering ship had dropped anchor in the Galveston harbor, which was bustling with activity. The *Independence* — flagship of the navy — was there, as well as the *Brutus*, which was undergoing repairs. The other two ships of the navy's fleet — the *Liberty* and *Invincible* — were out in the Gulf chasing down Mexican ships to loot. But they had not had much luck.

However, just when they were about to give up, our *Invincible* hit the jackpot. She destroyed the Mexican warship *Bravo* at the mouth of the Rio Grande. Hundreds of Mexicans were left helpless upon the beaches there. The Texans could not get on board this ship to capture the bounty because the water was too shallow for their ship.

But on that very same day it also captured the brig, *Pocket,* a ship of American registry, which was loaded to its gunwales with valuable supplies for the Mexican army.

70

When the word reached Burnet that the little navy steamer had scampered into Galveston Bay with all this loot, he could not help but feel better. And his face lightened with a smile. Piracy or semi-piracy, he felt that this was a good omen for Texas. And he wasted no time in dashing off another message to tell the Republic about the good news.

He was interrupted by someone knocking upon the door. A sailor boy informed him that his "Twin Sisters" from Cincinnati, Ohio, had arrived upon the steamer.

Burnet's mouth flew open. "What?" he asked.

"Your 'Twin Sisters,' sir," the lad replied, with a gleam in his eyes.

The president lit a shuck down to the dock, his coattails flapping in the wind. And his eyes went as round as silver dollars when he spied two identical, six-pound cannons.

Word spread as to what the new cargo really was, and how it was shipped in disguise as hollow ware to evade the neutrality laws of the United States. It drew those remaining in town like a magnet. Since they were the only field pieces of artillery that Texas had, all entered into a joyful celebration.

Burnet stood tall and straight; at the same time he looked deeply grateful and humble. He could not think of anything to say; he was so surprised. At least his friends from Cincinnati, where he used to practice law, had followed through. He wondered just how much his brother Isaax, who was the mayor of the city, had to do with this.

Then he hastened to reload the twins onto an ox-drawn wagon and sent them jogging along to Houston's camp up at Groce's. Oh, would they arrive in time to save Texas?

71

Sunday: April 10, 1836

It was a miserable day. There was a cold drizzle. Heavy black clouds were building up in the north. And it looked as if a storm would arrive any minute.

The first streaked light of dawn found the many homeless settlers up and shivering in their soggy clothes. They hurriedly went about the task of starting campfires to cook a quick breakfast before the oncoming storm.

The flickering fires showed their bleak, sad faces that were blue and pinched with cold. Many a one, no doubt, had thoughts of better times — when there were plenty of hot biscuits and butter, along with bacon and steaming mugs of coffee, also the comforts of a home with warm, dry clothes and a good bed to sleep in.

The norther soon hit. It picked up speed and brought heavy downpours of rain. Ships had to be grounded. The risk of them capsizing with those scanty — though nonetheless valuable — supplies was not worth taking a chance. So the vessels had to ride it out in the muddy waters, which churned and splashed up over the decks.

Little, if any, progress was made that day toward the war effort.

Monday: April 11, 1836

There had been no letup of the weather. If any-

thing it had worsened. Many small boats had overturned. Things were going from bad to worse.

Tuesday: April 12, 1836

The wind spent itself out during the night. And
the rain had subsided, leaving only its trace of puddles in the village paths of Harrisburg. In spite of
the mud and water, the few remaining refugees were
slogging through with aimless strides.

Their faces were stricken with fear as they heard
the latest reports that were running rampant through
the capital, like a fire in the pine forest. Word was out
that scattering bands of women and children had been
attacked, then killed by the Mexican army. There
were untold horrors of how the victims had been
tortured and shot down in cold blood; and the tales
grew wilder and wilder with each telling. This time
for sure they would *all* be murdered.

Despair and sorrow were also tearing at the hearts
of Burnet, Hardeman, and Thomas; Zavala had
again returned home — he feared for his family because of him.

Likely those reports were not all based on actual
facts. But there was no time to check them out. The
officers struggled among themselves on what stand to
take next. They knew something had to be done to
put an end to the terrifying situation. Heretofore,
they had felt reasonably safe here — but not anymore — with Santa Anna so close on their heels.

It was finally decided that Thomas would take
his turn in trying to make Houston fight. This time
he wrote the general a hot letter, which said in so

73

many words that the enemy was only one day's march away; that the chips were down; that he — Houston — had to put up or shut up; and furthermore, he must meet the enemy head on now or get the hell out — no two ways about it.

Houston was several days away from them. By a strange coincidence, he was crossing over onto the right bank of the Brazos River, using the steamer *Yellow Stone* and a small sailboat, on this same day. Does he plan to overtake Santa Anna and fight it out? Or is he, too, making an exodus — like the refugees — to the United States?

Questions, questions, questions!

Wednesday: April 13, 1836

David Burnet called the fragmented Horseback Government men together this morning, which consisted only of David Thomas and Bailey Hardeman. The time had come for them to leave Harrisburg. The decision as to where — hung heavy over his head. Galveston, maybe?

He had slept fitfully during the night. And when he arose from his dreary on-again, off-again naps, he found himself with a splitting headache — the likes of which had never troubled him before. He wondered how he would make the day through.

He dressed in his best Sunday-go-to-meeting suit, trying to look as dignified and calm as possible in his long shabby coat, under which there was slung two loaded pistols. Outwardly, he appeared calm — a trait he had learned from the Comanches when he lived with them on the sun-baked plains to take the cure for consumption. Today it is known as tuber-culosis.

For not only had they taught him how to hunt and track game, he had also learned how to remain cool when facing a dangerous enemy. By the time his blood-flecked cough had stopped they had also ingrained in him that life and death usually depended upon split-second timing.

Tension and an oppressive sun hung over the little capitol. All the doors and windows were open to catch any single breath of the hot, humid air. The slightest noise outside turned their heads. More times than once, they reached for their pistols as they turn-ed their ears to the slightest noises, like jangling spurs and clacking hoofbeats, or muttering of strange voices.

Most of the time they talked in low, audible tones. But sometimes hot words would flare up be-tween them, for their nerves were on edge and they knew their time was running out. However, those short outbursts did not last long. They were deter-mined to stick together, through thick and thin, and lick the oncoming oppressor.

They weighed the pros and cons of evacuation and finally came up with the plan of going to Galves-ton, after all. They reasoned that the barren island was the safest place to carry on the government. They also felt that they could run the blockade for sup-plies much easier there than by remaining on the mainland.

After the preliminaries were settled and Harde-man and Thomas were assigned their duties, Burnet went in to tell Mrs. Jane Harris good-by. A few of her friends were helping her pack. She was so poised

75

and seemingly unafraid as she sorted out some of her most treasured possessions.

This was one of the things he had been dreading — and now it had come. He was a timid soul when it came to dealing with women. He felt all tied up in knots and sweat stood upon his forehead. How could he say good-by to this noble woman who had not only turned her home over to the Horseback Government but had also stayed on to make things more comfortable for them. No doubt about it, she loved the town and the town loved her. And what was more, she was a true patriot for the Texas cause.

He cleared his throat but words of his planned speech had left him. He had so wanted it to be a proper and fitting farewell. He looked at her but the words stuck in his throat. So he just held out his hand and as their hands gripped, a brief thanks came out. She gave him an understanding smile.

Then the founding father of the Republic mounted up and rode away to move his family out of their home. He sat tall in his saddle as he waved his last good-by. Doubts were in his mind as to whether he would ever make it back here. Grim thoughts of death and defeat — Davy Crockett, Bowie, Fannin — were uppermost in his mind. He was well aware that he was racing against time.

Instead of returning to Harrisburg, the Burnets went swooping down to a nearby point at the head of Galveston Bay, called New Washington. This was the place that James Morgan had just recently started to develop. A few buildings had been erected, such as a hotel and a large warehouse. It was former-ly known as Clopper's Point.

This threw a monkey wrench into the plans of the land speculators, who were still using disruption

76

to fatten their holdings. These greedy, land-hungry operators went looking for Burnet at Harrisburg to secure another grant of land; this time they had their eyes on the uninhabited Galveston Island and Point Bolivar. They were miffed because they missed him; also Hardeman and Thomas turned thumbs down on their proposition.

Back up on the Brazos River, Houston had just about completed his crossover of wagons, ox teams and horses, along with the troops and their baggage, despite the rising tide. They were camping a few hundred yards east of Jared Groce's house. All were overjoyed over the "Twin Sisters" cannon that had just arrived.

Thursday: April 14, 1836

Believe it or not, Gen. Sam Houston had actually started maneuvers! His "boys" were running here and there and getting their arms in readiness. One wonders what part the secretary of the army, Tom Rusk, had in this.

Santa Anna had apparently decided against the idea of pursuing Houston's army any further. He was going for the Horseback Government instead.

The Mexican general got the word that these men were still in Harrisburg and he was out to get them personally. His mighty army had marched long and hard all day. And they were primed for the kill.

Hardeman and Thomas were still in Harrisburg. And Burnet planned to return there as soon as he got his family settled in New Washington. Zavala was also due to return at any minute. Could it be that these men were falling into the trap, after all? And this was the president's birthday.

Friday: April 15, 1836

There was a fog early this morning in New Washington. The sky was gray with low overhanging clouds. Only the faintest streaks of color were beginning to show through to indicate the position of the soon-to-be-rising sun.

David Burnet was in the saddle again riding along beside the sandy shore. He scarcely noticed the flamingos that were standing on their stemlike legs — or the swans as they arched their slender necks at the sound of his snorting horse. He just stared gloomily up the path that would eventually lead him to Harrisburg. He hoped to rejoin his three fellow officers there for last minute details of the evacuation.

To get there, he first had to go to the right a little and then veer to the left. This would take him to Vince's Bayou, which ran into Buffalo Bayou, where he could swing west for his destination. He felt fairly safe for there was good cover most of the way.

There was one stretch of prairie, however, which would openly expose him to the enemy. He would just have to take his chances of making it through safely.

When he reached this treeless tract of land, he halted his horse to scout the countryside. He had such an eerie feeling, as he twisted and turned around and then started up again. But so far there was not a thing to be alarmed about — only the pesky mosquitoes were around, and there were plenty of them. It was just that stillness that haunted him. Besides, it was no Sunday school picnic to be hunted like a criminal.

He was so weary as he trudged across. There was only one satisfaction — he would soon have this part of the journey over with.

Then suddenly he stopped. He heard noises and it wasn't a bear lumbering through the nearby forest, either. It sounded like a whole army clop-clopping forward. "I'm trapped," he thought.

He reached for his gun as he spotted the riders. What good could he do — one man against so many? He had been set up for a killing. On second thought — why would they be coming out in the open like that?

Then just as he raised his gun, he heard one of them yell out his name. David — why the enemy would not call him that, he reasoned. So he held off on the firing.

As they came closer, he could see they were his money-loaning acquaintances. "Thank God — even for speculators," he said, half out loud.

He rode out to meet them and he saw fear in their brazen faces. Something else dreadful had happened back at the capital. He knew by his instincts. Was it all over?

"They're coming!" one shouted.

"Woods is working alive with Mexicans," another called out.

Burnet listened, stiff in his saddle, as they informed him that all the people had just left out on the *Cayuga* — which was due to come downstream at any time. They suggested that he wait on shore with them and they would all catch it as it came by.

There was not any other choice. So he wasted no time in sending his servant back with all their horses. By the time the sun was hanging high in the sky, the men had boarded the steamer. Smaller open boats were bobbing up and down behind them. It was a solemn-looking procession.

The speculators could not refrain from presenting their latest proposition to the president as they churned on down toward Lynchburg. He listened but turned thumbs down on their scheme.

But his refusal failed to sink into the heads of these thick-skinned men. They kept picking and reminding him coyly that the government had made a legitimate agreement with them to get the land of their choosing for the money loaned in good faith. And a deal was a deal.

Burnet was so beaten down now with the woes of the revolution that it was difficult to resist them. He agreed half-heartedly — with the understanding that he must first consult with the others in private.

After the officers went onshore to spend the night in Lynchburg, they weighed the pros and cons of these demands. Finally, all consented to sign — but for only one section of land instead of the two that had been asked for. They called these men in for a showdown.

Burnet concluded wearily by saying, "Get one thing through your heads, men — this is the last time. I don't want to hear any more out of you about this."

Back at Harrisburg: The Mexican soldiers were even closer on the heels of the Texans than any had suspected. Just after sundown they sneaked in on the village. Shadowy figures slinked among the cabins

80

with the intent of slipping up on the Horseback officers so they could capture them. But no such luck.

All they found were three printers, who had just moved in from San Felipe and managed to put out an edition of the *Telegraph and Texas Register*. One can easily imagine how furious Santa Anna was over the *norteamericanos* giving him the slip. Knowing him, he would not give up on them.

After questioning the printers to find the whereabouts of these so-called revolutionary officers of Texas, the Mexican general dumped their printing press into the bayou. Then he put the torch to the town. Blood-red sparks and flames were lapping and leaping into the night-leaden sky.

Saturday: April 16, 1836

The Horseback Government men had to hang up their saddles and take to riding the waves. The *Cayuga* was taking them this morning to the new capital at Galveston — away from Santa Anna, who was on the verge of catching up with them again at Lynchburg.

Burnet thought over the plans they had made to move on down. There was much about them that he did not like but he could not come up with anything better. As the side-wheeler left, Burnet was determined not to look back. "Ever onward and up," he said, as he raised his head to the heavens.

Despite his outward calm, he was far from confident, as he consulted with the captain over a map. "Drop me off here at New Washington." Then he pointed to the village of Anahuac. "Zigzag across the

81

bay to here," he said, "and let the settlers off. It is a safe place to go; and perhaps it would be easier to get to the United States from there — most of them are bound for there, anyhow."

"Here," he pointed to the northeastern tip on a narrow ribbon of land which touched the Gulf of Mexico on its far side, "is our new capital. Take Zavala, Thomas, and Hardeman there as quickly as you can. I'll join them later, as soon as I can pick up my family."

As soon as the *Cayuga* let the president off it picked up full speed ahead. Sad-faced passengers were swaying aimlessly with the movement of the boat. Horrifying reports were floating around ninety knots to nothing — about how the Mexicans were closing in fast and completely encircling the bay. Who knew — perhaps they were waiting at Anahuac to cut them down. Oh, if Houston would only get here.

Times were getting so perilous that no one dared to venture out unarmed. The captain had the two guns of his ship ready to fire at a moment's notice. Men were putting their firearms in readiness. Some were measuring gunpowder from their horns. Others were cleaning or loading shotguns. A few were carelessly hefting their loaded pistols and aiming, as if to fire.

David Thomas was busy polishing off his elegant pistol. The attorney general — now also acting as secretary of war since Rusk was still with Houston — took great care of his favorite weapon. It had gone with him on all his travels.

Then suddenly, someone fired a shot. All heads turned in the same direction from where the sound came.

"It's Thomas!" a voice cried out.

82

"Oh, my God, he's been shot!" someone next to him shouted.

Sure enough it was David Thomas. His face was gray and grim. He stared down at the blood that was seeping through his pants leg and dripping to the deck. Then his eyes glazed and he slumped over into unconciousness.

His leg was shattered by a bullet that went wild. From all accounts it sounded like an accident, since no one claimed to have actually seen the happening. But it is strange that an expert gunman like David Thomas would accidentally shoot himself. The doctor on board was having great difficulty in stopping the flow of blood.

Sunday: April 17, 1836

The overcast sky was as gloomy and gray as the mood of the few remaining Texans who were down at the warehouse in New Washington. They were stacking baggage and making ready to board the steamer at the nearby wharf when it arrived.

It was so hot and sultry. Not a breath of air was stirring inside. It was depressing as though the dampness in the air carried a warning. David Burnet, with his wife, Hannah, and also the boys — William and Jacob — were there.

The president was helping his friend, Dr. George Patrick, and a Negro servant with the sorting. He had scarcely started when he heard a clanking of hoofs. He swung around half-crouched and looked out the door.

It was his own personal servant. What was wrong? Burnet pondered and could not make out the reason for such a quick return. He had just sent that Negro back earlier this morning to pick up a valise, which had been left in the shuffle during the fast exit from their home the other day.

The rider lost no time. He slid from his horse and hit the ground running. "The Mexicans are coming!" he said, panting for breath.

"What?" Burnet stopped, dead still.

"Yes, sir, Master Burnet. They'se done cleaned out the Zavalas — and they'se com' this way. Hurry, Master, hurry!"

Burnet had no doubts as to the boy's sincerity. He had been rather half-expecting such in the back of his mind. And the steamer wasn't here. There was no time to wait for it. Why did he let the *Cayuga* go? Why didn't he delay it long enough to fetch his family while he still had the chance to leave? Why — why — oh, why did he put off like this?

There was no way — no place to hide. He scanned the bayscape, looking with careful eyes, as if half-expecting to see the side-wheeler. His eyes blurred from the strain.

Then he caught sight of a rowboat on the beach. His heart gave a leap. It looked so small down there. But they could all squeeze in somehow. They must go to it at once.

He spun around and faced the silent group. They were looking to him for an answer. "Let's make it for the boat down there."

Burnet tucked baby Jacob under his arm and turned to Dr. Patrick. "George, can you manage William?"

84

"Sure," said the doctor, lifting the child up into his arms.

The president grabbed hold of his wife and they side-stepped the baggage on their way out. He could not help but notice — even in this state of confusion and fear — how sad Hannah looked as she cast one last fleeting glimpse toward a certain bundle on the floor. It contained a few of her favorite things that she had skimped and saved up for since their arrival to their Texas home.

Burnet flushed at the thoughts of another time when she had looked this way and had lost all in that ill-fated shipwreck. He vowed to himself to make it up to her someday, as he tightened his arm around her. Together, they made it down the trail and into the boat.

Clouds hung heavy in the darkened sky above the cramped little crew. Sea gulls called in their plaintive way and circled overhead, as if warning that all was not well on this Sabbath day.

Suddenly, one of the Negro oarsmen stopped paddling. "Master!" he shot out with the force of desperation and pointed back to the bank.

The president whirled. His eyes went searching. In an instant, he saw someone topping a rise — then another — and another. Now the sound of shouting voices.

Within minutes, there were surly brown faces everywhere he turned. Then a sudden halt near the water's edge; they were no more than thirty yards away from the departing boat.

Burnet was sick with fear. It was his duty to do something. He started to reach for his gun. But he knew that would mean sudden death. So he dropped his hand back down to his side.

The Mexican leader stepped out in front of his troops. It was Col. Juan Almonte. Burnet recognized him; he was that notorious, half-breed informer that had been keeping Santa Anna posted about the Texans.

Almonte took a short step nearer, his hand on the butt of his gun. He jerked his gun from its holster.

And on a sudden impulse, Burnet jumped to his feet. He knew what he must do. He leaped to the back of the boat and took a stance. With his body he attempted to screen his loved ones from the bullets.

He made a perfect target as he stood there in his long black coat. His military posture, broad shoulders and wide, bearded face — that might have been chipped of stone — was enough to mark him anywhere.

"He'll shoot over my dead body," Burnet said, swaying back and forth with the rocking boat.

"Row," he stormed out at the oarsmen. "Row! George, hold on to the children!"

"Davy," Hannah sobbed, jerking on his coattail. "Get down."

He did not even feel the weight of her tugging. He just strove to maintain his balance and keep his eyes on the Mexicans.

Almonte was aiming, taking a steady bead on Burnet. He was a fast one with a gun — speedier than Santa Anna, so some of the tales went.

But suddenly, he stopped and slowly lowered his gun. He gave a shouting command in Spanish and the troops moved back a little.

Burnet could not believe his eyes as he drifted away safely and watched the enemy disappear out of his sight. It was a long time before they loosened up. For the most part they just sat silently. Burnet was

86

so puzzled over what had just happened. It was certainly a new slant from the no-quarters policy that the Mexicans had followed during the revolution. It could mean anything — or nothing.

Little did he know that Almonte had spotted Hannah hunched down in the boat. Whatever else he might be, the colonel had respect for a woman. He had held his fire because the bullet might ricochet and hit Hannah instead. Only that prevented some more bloody murders — on a Sunday.

The refugees were beginning to collect their wits and an almost serene peace lay over them, despite the incident and the oncoming storm. The oarsmen resumed a more normal speed of rowing for they were exhausted.

But back behind them another drama was taking place and not too far off either. A large boat was coming rapidly from up the bay. Little William spotted it. "Look-ee," he pointed, "a big boat."

"Oh, no," they gasped.

But sure enough in the distance a boat was appearing. So it was a trap after all, Burnet concluded. They are closing in to take us all alive. He was sick. Fear and tension were mounting with the high onrushing waves.

The recollection of how Fannin and his men had surrendered, how they had been shot down in cold-blooded murder, when they thought they were being set free — jabbed him inside.

The boat was coming closer. Now it was swinging over toward the refugees. The waves were splashing up over the skiff, filling it with water and drenching them as well. It looked as if they would capsize any minute.

"They won't take me alive," Burnet said. "I'll kill myself first."

"Me, too," wailed Hannah. "I'll jump — and take my children with me."

The president pulled out his dagger. Just as he aimed the point at his body, the oncoming ship gave a toot. Burnet twisted, his face as pale as a sheet.

"Master, them's white folks on that ship."

"Yes, I know," whispered Burnet, as he lowered his weapon limply. "Providence is on our side."

The captain picked them up and then they headed out for Galveston Island. It was pouring down rain, thunder roared, and lightning crackled all around. They were a drippy and dejected-looking bunch — but they were alive. And what was more precious than that?

Monday: April 18, 1836

The first family was still on the ship, which had dropped anchor at Galveston Island. They were remaining on board for a while just in case there was a necessity for further retreat. Each member was worn out from the traumatic experiences of the previous day. William and Jacob had runny noses and were fussy. Hannah spent most of her time with them.

The president — despite his stiff joints and sore muscles — had worked most of the day reassembling important papers. This was the last hope for helping Texas. Problems were falling fast and heavy upon his shoulders.

He was so discouraged. Never a kind word ever

seemed to fall his way anymore. He was blamed for the way the revolution was going and anything else that came up. Being highly sensitive, each remark cut him deeper to the bone. He felt as if he was about slashed to pieces.

Too, he was so concerned over David Thomas, who was still in a bad way. They had done the best they could for him during these times. He had lost so much blood that his strength was ebbing away. And now gangrene had set in. His leg had swollen to almost twice its normal size.

He just lay there, breathing hard and moaning, sometimes muttering in inaudible tones. He probably wouldn't last the night through.

It was hard to watch a good man go. Burnet recollected the early morning hour when Thomas was sworn in as the attorney general of the Horseback Government back in Washington-on-the-Brazos. This seemed so long ago but actually it had been only a mite over a month.

He and Thomas had talked a lot about freedom and peace and Texas since then. But they seldom discussed the past. Consequently, the president knew very little about his fellow officer's personal life. However, that was not important as to who or what he was — nor where; he was a loyal patriot, interested in the freedom of his newly adopted country — and that was what counted.

There had been just one tiny ray of hope to shine through that day. Houston was then gaining on Santa Anna; he was within the present-day city limits of Houston. Santa Anna was down below a bit, around Vince's Bayou, and headed on toward New Washington. He was still searching for our Horseback G-men.

Tuesday: April 19, 1836

Galveston Island is a long silvery strip of sand that arches out into the Gulf of Mexico, along the upper stretches of the Texas coast. It is no more than three miles at the widest part and often much narrower. The contour of the shell-studded beaches and cozy little coves varies with the storms of the season.

There are many stories and legends about this low-lying island. It was originally the home of the Karankawa Indians, who roved the dunes and ridges in search for food. This might have included berries and nuts, or oysters and fish from the bays, such as redfish, whiting, trout, and croakers, or perhaps a white captive for their *piéce de résistance*.

The first arrivals were the Spaniards, who sailed across the ocean seeking fame and fortune for their homeland. They were often shipwrecked — Cabeza de Vaca, for one — and washed ashore. Many others were less fortunate and ended up on the shallow bottoms offshore within their sunken ships.

It has since been occupied by other adventurers, such as the swashbuckling buccaneer known as Jean Lafitte; he used the island as a hideout and a place to bury his stolen treasure. Too, it has been said that even the fabulous, ill-fated Frenchman named La Salle dropped anchor here for a time before sailing off down the coast.

That day, in the spring of 1836, Galveston Island was a desolate-looking place. There were only a few gnarled trees and scattered brush with patches

90

of sharp-bladed salt grass here and there. All that remained to remind one of its historic past were pieces of broken glass and crockery, along with rusty nails and drift logs.

There was one small deserted building, which was used as the custom house by the Mexicans. They tried to charge the settlers tax on goods which were shipped in — like the British and the tea in the American Revolution. But the Texans would not stand for it. So they ran the hombres off.

However barren it appeared to be, it was now the refuge of the Horseback Government — the last stronghold for the fledgling Republic. David Burnet and his diminishing cabinet (Thomas passed away that day) were here; there were also quite a few fugitives who followed and some sixty soldiers to man the island.

A dense fog had slipped in silently and was drifting over the dejected little gathering. Normally, on a clear day one could see over the entire point on this eastern tip. Now, all they could see were the sand dunes, heaped by wind and wave, and ghostly looking clumps of driftwood.

In the distance were the plaintive cries of sea birds — the crane, curlew, and gull — who sound wild and shrill and uncanny. And closer by was the splat of the restless, whitecapped waves as they broke upon the shore, and the shifty sand that crunched underfoot as the refugees went about their tasks of settling-in for the duration.

Burnet looked across over to the mainland. He asked himself — Where is that notorious Santa Anna? Is he still shaking the bushes for us?

The president of course was unaware that the Mexican general had given up finding the slippery

G-men; that he had put the torch to New Washington, after having the warehouse ransacked for supplies, and was backtracking toward Lynchburg and Buffalo Bayou, burning every house or dwelling that he cast his eyes upon along the trail.

Obviously, it seemed that this manhunt had marked the beginning of the Mexican general's undoing. For upon such tactics as this, revolutions can be lost — or won.

The president turned his eyes toward the Gulf. Somewhere out there were the enemy's fleet of ships. It was such an eerie feeling to be socked in by the fog and to be completely surrounded by the enemy. It was enough to unnerve any man.

Whatever was going to happen would happen fast now. He had just received word that Houston was a little over two miles below Harrisburg; the general left his baggage and the sick soldiers back on the banks of Buffalo Bayou — across from the charred ruins of Harrisburg.

Slowly, it came to him that all was not lost. They had to keep the supply lines open to Houston and choke off Santa Anna from his.

He hastened to send over a note to Robert Potter, urging him to tighten up on the blockade. If this could be done, the navy secretary was the one that could do it; he never ceased to marvel at that man's capabilities — if only he would leave the women alone.

The president then sent the *Cayuga* on its way to Houston, loaded with scanty provisions and some volunteers who had come from the United States. If they made it through the fog and the enemy — well — that was almost too much to hope for.

Wednesday: April 20, 1836

Great throngs of homeless women and children (brown, black, and white), money lenders and speculators, even some signers of the Declaration of Independence, were fleeing into the United States. They were up to here with the tragic tales of the Alamo and Goliad, as well as the wild rumors that Santa Anna was on their heels, coupled with the feeling that Houston had failed them. All of this together had been more than they could stand. By dark, Texas would be a deserted wasteland.

The only ones left to care for their newly adopted homeland were the scrubby little army on the banks of Buffalo Bayou and the members of the Horseback Government, who were on Galveston Island with a handful of their loyal followers.

Under a cloudy, leaden-gray sky that was tinged with blood-red streaks of the rising sun, the government men were building emergency shelters on the island. Some were pulling the tops of waist-high grasses together and joining them with strands of reeds, which were also used to weave through, for reinforcements. If they were lucky enough to get some logs of driftwood they had it made.

Most of the fugitives were sleeping on the sandy beaches, with no beds or bedding. All their household furnishings — including those of the first family — were left behind and were now in ashes.

Others were rousting around for some sticks to make a fire to boil water for coffee and to cook their scanty rations. Luckily, the place was inhabited with

93

deer for venison, also birds and their eggs — which were to be found for the gathering in hollowed-out nests amid the shells and slick little pebbles back from the shoreline. Like their tattooed, red-skinned brothers, they also had to learn to subsist upon oysters and fish from the salty waters.

President Burnet was busy slapping mosquitoes and dashing off more urgent pleas for help to the people in the United States, many of which were in New Orleans. He decided he must urge Potter to confiscate all goods that were usable for the army, but to make a note of all the takes so they could eventually reimburse the owners. He was still an optimistic soul.

Gen. Sam Houston and Secretary of War Tom Rusk were in the woods just opposite Santa Anna's camp. The two Texas leaders had already made stirring speeches to an overly anxious, get-on-with-it group of troops.

Their battle cry was "Remember the Alamo! Remember Goliad! Victory at San Jacinto!" There was going to be a shoot-out — come the following day!

Thursday: April 21, 1836

The morning mist had cleared away, leaving a brassy sun shining down upon General Houston's ragtag troops. They were less than a mile from Gen. Santa Anna and his dapper, well-equipped soldiers at the junction of Buffalo Bayou and San Jacinto River. Houston was in a fringe of woods behind a grassy knoll, while Santa Anna was on higher ground

94

overlooking the marshes. An open prairie lay between the two camps.

The Texans had been ready to start the shooting ever since daylight. In fact, they had been champing at the bits ever since the preliminary skirmish the day before, which Houston put a stop to in no uncertain terms.

With the exception of the fresh recruits that had arrived that morning from Galveston at the direction of President Burnet, most of them had spent over a month on the trail retreating and camping out in the wet, windy weather. Their bitter feelings — left over from the Alamo and Goliad — rankled and the resentment that lay buried deep within each and every one was erupting to the surface. There was no quit in these angry revolutionaries that day.

By midmorning they had scouted the Mexicans from some nearby treetops and no one seemed to be out of their tents. Surely, "His Excellency" must be around somewhere. They believed that he would attack them before the day was over or make some kind of move soon, for he had thrown up a breastwork of bags, baggage, saddles, and sacks of provisions for protection. Also, General Cós had just arrived by way of Vince's Bridge from the Brazos River area with over four hundred additional troops; this was the second time around in Texas for him.

When Houston learned of this he spat tobacco juice on the ground and let out an oath, then said, "I'll put a stop to that. Deaf Smith, come over here."

He summoned tough, loyal Erastus (Deaf) Smith to burn that bridge, posthaste. Smith gathered his men together and left out.

This bridge burning would work both ways, though. There was no chance for anybody to leave now — Texans or Mexicans. It was a showdown to go forward into battle and fight — win, lose, or draw. Houston had staked his life and his men upon this decision. This was truly their darkest hour.

The general went about setting up his strategy for the onslaught as thick coils of smoke curled skyward from the burning bridge. Deaf Smith had completed his mission and should return soon.

By midafternoon — around 3:30 P.M. — Houston called his officers together and ordered them to get their men ready. All quietly took their places in the battle line. The cavalry spread out on the wings — Tom Rusk was on the left side. The "Twin Sisters" were wheeled into center position. The infantry marched in and flanked the cannon on both sides. The youthful color guard lined up carrying the white silk battle flag, its gold fringe trim shimmering in the sun, and as the banner waved in the breeze it revealed the painted figure of a beautiful lady whose hand was grasping a sword — over which was draped a streamer with the words "Liberty or Death"; the long lady's party glove tied to the staff was a reminder of happier times back in Kentucky.

Where the Texans stood the ground was flat but it swelled slowly up to a grassy mound about a quarter of a mile away from their enemy. Such a site was deceptive and although it seemed open, a surprise attack was possible in just such a terrain.

There was a risk involved, however. Undoubtedly, most would be taking a *siesta* (an afternoon nap), but a few would be awake to alert the others. So the best and only way was to charge quickly — like greased lightning — before they realized what was actually happening.

Houston gave his command to advance from his

96

great white stallion. All marched silently out of the low ground, over the rim and out into the open prairie — where there was no protection. They now faced an archenemy whose numbers they did not know, except that they were quite sure to be greater than their own.

"Fire!" Houston shouted. "Fire away!"

Suddenly, the fifers and a drummer struck up with the tune of the times — "Will You Come to My Bower" — only to be drowned out by loud bangs, one after another, after another. The "Twin Sisters" roared as they belched out broken horseshoes, nails, and whatever else the cannoneers loaded them with.

They lay down an artillery barrage, killing as many as possible; the infantry moved up rapidly as the battle became fully engaged; the cavalry put the spurs to their horses and went crashing in from the wings, whooping and yelling "Remember the Alamo! Remember Goliad!"

Above the din and roar, Tom Rusk shouted out, "Give 'em hell, boys!"

Then Santa Anna's forces were hit on both sides, forcing them back deeper and deeper into the quagmire of marshes along the bayou. The very ferocity of the attack demoralized the Mexican army, breaking them into splinter groups and destroying their leadership.

Mexican soldiers — made up mostly of peons and ex-convicts — ran for the swamps and across the prairie toward Vince's Bridge. Eighteen minutes of crashing, plunging, shouting, shooting, slashing — then it was over, in less time than it takes to read about it.

Texan casualties were light, among which was Sam Houston. His stallion was shot out from under him and his ankle was shattered by a rifle ball. But he took to a riderless horse, and then another, swinging his leg over the saddle horn as he rode on with his men. The Mexicans lost heavily — somewhere in the hundreds.

Though the battle was over, there was no way of stopping the vengeful Texans — once they got started. Not even Houston could hold them back now. They killed and pillaged; they rounded up horses and mules, captured supplies of camp equipment and arms — including pistols, sabers, and muskets — and confiscated an elegant military chest that was filled to the brim with some twelve thousand dollars in silver, which was more money than they had ever seen in their whole lifetime.

This kept on until the night closed in around the exhausted victors. Then the silvery moon and the twinkling stars took over, casting their ghostly lights upon the prairie, which softened the gory site of one of the shortest, strangest, and perhaps most significant battles in the history of the world.

Texas was free at last!

Friday: April 22, 1836

Many Mexicans, including Santa Anna, escaped in the darkness the day before. Houston was aware of this and he was concerned. He couldn't overlook the possibility that the wily Mexican general might try to rally his depleted army and make a comeback.

The injured Texas general wasted no time this morning in calling his men to the open-air headquarters, which was under a spreading live oak tree in the middle of the battleground. His six-foot plus, sturdily built frame was sprawled out on a pallet. He was using a saddle as his prop and tried to make himself as comfortable as possible with that bad ankle. He was good looking in a rough-and-tumble sort of way.

"Boys," the blunt-speaking and hard-driving Houston said, "round up every Mexican you can find. Santa Anna's still running loose. Find the bloody murderer and bring him back here to me."

He detected a restlessness in his undisciplined troops that he did not like. He could tell by the glints in their eyes and the scowls upon their faces what they were up to.

So he looked them straight in their eyes and thundered out, "But mind you — no more killing. And be damned sure that you bring Santa Anna back alive. He has to be the one to negotiate complete surrender. I'll personally deal with anyone who violates this order, hear?"

The scrappy fighters agreed and everyone that could get a pack mule or horse rode out over the countryside. More than a few loped off to Vince's Bayou, about eight miles away.

Most of the fugitives had headed there to make their getaway after the battle. When they found that the bridge was down, they either attempted to swim across (this was when so many got picked off the previous day by the Texans), or they took to the tall timbers and high grass.

As they were discovered many begged for mercy, crying out, "Me no Alamo; me no Goliad" — meaning that they had no part in these massacres. But the Texans paid them no mind.

They rounded up Mexicans by the hundreds

99

and hustled them into the outdoor POW camp, which was heavily patrolled — also guarded by the "Twin Sisters," which were loaded and ready to shoot. Anyone making a break to escape would be blown to bits.

The hardheaded Texans adhered to their general's rule of no killing. But with thoughts of the Alamo and Goliad still so fresh upon their minds, they were not above using the butts of their guns to strike the captives if they did not walk as fast as they thought they should, or to giving them a good tongue lashing. This was lost on most of the Mexicans, however, since they "No savvy de English."

Colonel Almonte was the only prisoner who could speak our language very well; he had learned how as a student in the United States. So he answered all the questions that Tom Rusk asked pertaining to names of the captured and their ranks.

You will recall Almonte was the one that could have shot President Burnet at New Washington but didn't. Now his own life had been spared. Some said that Tom Rusk was responsible for his safety; it was the group with the secretary of war that captured the colonel the day before and marched him back to camp unharmed.

Lorenzo de Zavala, Jr. had been brought in off the battlefield to assist as an interpreter, since he was fluent in both languages — thanks to his father, the vice-president.

The Zavala family home nearby had been set up as an emergency hospital. Bandages torn from available sheets and rags, and a few tins of salve had been divided among the Texans for dressing their wounds. About all that could be raked and scraped together to feed them were some hard biscuits and dried beef.

100

Later, the wounded enemy soldiers would be brought here. They would have to be laid end to end on every floor of the house for there was many a one out there sick and dying. This would have to be soon or it would be too late for most of them. Some of the Texans had been assigned to sort the injured enemy out and gather them in. But while they went about doing this they also did not miss a bet to add to their loot collection.

These men returned to camp with wagons loaded down. It has been said that their bounty included Santa Anna's silver-studded saddle and his sword; also his elegant camp furniture, such as a silver tea set, monogramed china, cut glass tumblers and ornately etched decanters with golden stoppers — along with plenty of champagne to fill them. (Someone remarked that if Santa Anna had not been partying with a pretty slave girl, he might not have lost the battle — but that is neither here nor there.)

They also wheeled in the dictator's bedding, and his decorated chamber pot. Now what rough-and-tumble Texas soldier would be caught dead using that fancy thing?

The Texans came in looking like a walking arsenal. It was not uncommon for a man to be seen packing as many pistols as he could strap around his waist or stick inside his belt, a knapsack bulging with bullets, several powder horns swinging around his neck, and as many rifles and muskets as he could carry off in his arms. This was a rich find to many a soldier who had never in his whole lifetime ever had more than one old and worn, hand-me-down squirrel gun in his possession at any given time.

The biggest and most valuable prize for all Texans at that moment, however, would be to find Santa

Anna. Our scrappy soldiers had been hot on his trail ever since sunup. They had combed the bushes and his whereabouts was still unknown.

One bunch (so the story goes) decided to go for game instead. They spotted some bucks and a doe grazing in the clearing and they decided to bring in some camp meat for the day. They were drooling over the prospect of having venison steaks for supper. (There was no closed season in these days.)

The fellows hid out waiting for a good shot. But all of a sudden, the deer raised their heads and in a flash went bounding off with white tails waving in the air. Being good hunters, it did not take long for these men to figure out that something closer-in had frightened those deer away.

So they decided to take a look around. And sure enough they spied a Mexican stretched out and half-hidden in the tall grass. One of the men lowered his gun, since he was so put out over missing his shot at the deer. But his partner yelled for him to stop, reminding him about Houston's orders.

The men stepped from their saddles and onto the ground. About that time the fugitive jumped up. Since the Texans did not know any Spanish and the Mexican apparently did not know any English, they could not communicate. So they hastened him back to camp on horse and foot.

The captive was a scrubby, middle-aged man of medium size, dressed in a common, ordinary blue jacket and coarse white pants. One thing these Texans noticed, however, was that some fancy rigging — like a silk shirt — was sticking out from around his neck; and the sharp-pointed slippers that he was wearing did not seem to jive with the rest of his clothing.

They didn't think much about this at the time,

102

since clothes made no difference to these frontier back-woodsmen anyway. They just wore what was available and never really bothered about mixing or matching.

It was not until these men entered the camp that they began to suspect that this Mexican was no ordinary prisoner. He pulled away from them and started jabbering something that they could not make out. The only thing they could understand was the prattle about General Houston.

Then to cap it all off, one of the prisoners called out, "El Presidente!" and others joined in. You could have knocked these Texans over with a feather. It suddenly dawned on them that this man had to be Santa Anna. Now they knew the reason for the strange-looking combination of clothing.

El Presidente — General Santa Anna — was marched off toward Houston. Our soldiers crowded in around and taunted him as they followed. Dangerous tension was mounting with an undesirable mixture of bitterness and morbid curiosity. All were packing firearms and there was a savage look in their eyes. If Santa Anna so much as made a wrong turn, he would be assassinated so quickly that he would never know what had hit him.

"Hang him," a soldier shouted, flicking a rope and swinging it carelessly.

"Hangin's too good for the murderer," yelled a frontiersman in buckskins with a Bowie knife. "Slit his throat!"

"Take him back to Goliad — and shoot him down," hissed a strong, squarely built survivor of the Goliad massacre who was thirsting for revenge.

The captive staggered into camp, his face set in grim lines. He stood at attention before Sam Houston. This self-styled "Napoleon of the West" had little resemblance to the suave, bemedalled general with gold epaulettes upon his shoulders, who had detailed the bloody massacres of Fannin and Crockett, Bowie and Travis — to name a few. He was a disheveled mess in those cast-off clothes from his slippers and mud-splattered pants to the tip of his sweat-matted head.

The arrogant general clenched his hands into knotted fists. He was suffering the greatest humiliation of his life, having to knuckle under to rough, uncouth rebels — with Houston the epitome of all that.

There was contempt in his steely black eyes as he faced Houston and said, "Gen. Antonio López de Santa Anna, the president of the Republic of Mexico."

Burly Sam Houston, being a magnanimous conqueror, replied, "General Santa Anna, El Presidente, eh?"

He motioned with his hand for Santa Anna to sit beside him on an old war chest. Without a doubt Houston was adhering to the protocol of the articles of war on how to treat a prisoner. The general was even dressed for the occasion in formal attire. He waved his soldiers, who were still on the verge of turning this summit meeting into a mob scene, to step back for the interrogation.

The subject of other Mexican troops that were scattered over the country was uppermost in General Houston's mind, as well as in Colonel Rusk's. Gen. Vicente Filisola's group was reportedly only a short march away from there.

"I'm asking you to surrender all your troops,

General," Houston demanded with cold, calculating eyes.

The fallen general shifted from one foot to another, his eyes staring with brooding thoughts.

Then Tom Rusk, who was leaning up against the oak tree behind Houston, put in, "We'll have to do battle with Filisola, if you don't call him off."

Then Houston retracted his demand and said, "So, I ask you to *retire* your men."

This was done, perhaps, as an afterthought on Houston's part, for Texas had no place to house the prisoners, neither was there food or clothing to provide them with — if they *surrendered*.

Santa Anna raised his head to buzzards that were circling low. The smell of death was in the air. He looked around at the angry faces that were tensed for a hanging — and then lowered his head.

There was no way. If he had ever hoped to regroup with Filisola or General Urrea and plan another battle it was all over now. His own arrogance and brutality had trapped him in this hopeless situation. Losing Texas was as hard a blow to him as the loss of Russia had been to his idol, Napoleon Bonaparte. So the sullen general agreed to order Filisola and all the others to go back to Mexico immediately.

Deaf Smith was sitting directly across from Santa Anna on a stump, holding a gun in one hand and cupping his ear with the other. He was trying to make out what was going on. When the square-shouldered and stockily built New York-born Texan heard this, he jumped up and said, "Boss, let me git th' message to 'em."

Houston no doubt recalled to his mind the successes of this famous scout in the fringed buckskin jacket, including when he blocked the escape route

105

the day before — at just the right moment. There was no one he could send that knew the lay of the land or understood Mexicans like this middle-aged settler did. In fact he was married to a Mexican and at times he even looked like one.

The general turned his head toward Rusk to see what he had to say. Both nodded in agreement for Smith to take the first dispatch. (There were others that had to be sent to Filisola.)

After this long, nerve-wracking ordeal was over, Tom Rusk made a final check on the late arrivals in the prison camp. It had been a weary day and he was all in. He was ready to sack out.

Then suddenly, it came to him that David Burnet had not been notified of the battle nor the victory. So the secretary of war hastily jotted down the victory message to his loyal friend, the president of the Republic of Texas.

Saturday: April 23, 1836

Thomas Rusk ordered Benjamin C. Franklin, along with two other assistants, to carry the message about the victory at San Jacinto to Pres. David Burnet on Galveston Island. Also, at the last minute, Robert J. Calder volunteered to go with them; his girl friend, so he had learned by the grapevine, was among the refugees there.

They departed in a small leaky boat, which was the only one available for travel. It would be slow as they would have to wind along the shallow shoreline. Since there was no space left for food, they would have to go ashore and scrounge around among the empty houses for leftovers.

It was regrettable that Burnet had not already learned about the win. For at the moment he was a very despondent man. Lorenzo de Zavala had resigned (for reasons he said would be explained later) and shipped out on the army-bound *Cayuga*.

Burnet had already accepted the resignation with regrets. He was out on the point of the island trying to think things through. He cut a mighty lonely figure standing out there by himself, as he rubbed his tousled head of shaggy white hair. His face, with its stubble of white whiskers, was gaunt and lined with fatigue. The strain of the disappointment over Zavala showed in his eyes as he wondered how a man's life could get him into such exasperating circumstances.

He had thought that the vice-president was one man that he could always depend on. Oh, he knew the little Mexican could get fired up at the drop of his hat and start erupting at a moment's notice. But he usually calmed down just as quickly. They had managed to talk things over before and come to a satisfactory conclusion.

He realized that the man was discouraged. "But what about me," Burnet thought. "I am half-starved and wearing the only clothes that I possess in this world; and I have spent all my money. What's more, I have not received any salary for all this misery. What does it all add up to for me? Nothing. Maybe I ought to resign, too."

The president's mind meandered like the waters that put out to sea. He could not keep from wondering if Zavala would have stayed on had there been someone else at the helm.

"I know I'm not perfect — some say I am too formal and straitlaced because I cannot tolerate drinking and swearing; that I'm too conservative and am prone to put things off too long; and that I never joke or josh. That's mostly personal and a man has a right to live his own life. Things are serious with me, especially now — when a whole nation is at stake."

He listened to the waves as they splashed upon the beach. There was something so tranquil about the sound, like it came to wash away tears and heal the hurts. Suddenly, he heard someone calling back behind him.

"Chief, the new recruits are here. What'll I do with them?"

It was Bailey Hardeman. Burnet had almost forgotten about him. But the secretary of the treasury was very much on the job trying to help his leader with the gigantic tasks of the revolution; in fact he had taken on more and more duties as the cabinet diminished in number.

Burnet drew in a deep breath of fresh salty air. His body became more relaxed and the tenseness seemed to have drifted out of him.

"I'm coming, Bailey," the executive said in a calm, cool, deliberate voice. His iron-cast face broke into a smile as he walked toward the "President's House," which was a sparsely furnished, makeshift shelter of drift logs and clump grass.

Sunday: April 24, 1836

The "Runaway Scrape" folks were footsore, sunburned, and weary-worn. Food was getting scarcer day by day. If it was not for people like Erasmo Seguin — and thank goodness there were others — many a one would have starved by then. The loyal old patriarch, whose son commanded a Mexican cavalry unit in Houston's army, had shepherded his flock of some three thousand sheep along the grassy plains to provide meat for all those who were hungry.

A group of tired and heavy-laden stragglers, who were still in Texas, had just heard some news from an unknown courier that Houston had fought with the Mexicans — and won. They just shook their heads. It was likely there had been a battle all right but as to Houston being the winner — they had their doubts. They paid the messenger no heed and trudged on toward the east.

Those on the island had not even had that much of a trace in regards to the good news. They were growing more restless by the hour, and were seriously thinking of shipping out for New Orleans.

Monday: April 25, 1836

Sam Houston settled down long enough that day to write out an official report on the Battle of San Jacinto of Thursday, April 21, 1836. The commander in chief made himself as comfortable as possible with his bad ankle and addressed the message to his Excellency D. G. Burnet, president of the Republic of Texas.

He penned the word *Sir* — then started off by saying he was sorry that he had not sent an official report of the victory sooner but he had been so busy that he had not taken the time to do so.

He got right into the preliminaries prior to the battle, beginning when they started tracking Santa Anna down on the eighteenth; how they successfully captured a Mexican trooper, who was persuaded to tell that his general and the one crack division with him was headed to Anahuac in a leisurely pace, and if the Texans would push on with all speed throughout the night as well as the next day, they should catch up with them somewhere near Lynch's Ferry — which they did.

With a flourish he detailed the news about the skirmish the day before the battle and in bold strokes of the pen he pointed out that his men had won. He mentioned that Santa Anna was probably thinking he would have a much better position if he would withdraw to the San Jacinto River at its confluence of Buffalo Bayou, where he would have his back and flanks protected by the water. Anyway, he began fortifying his position there.

After scouting the enemy and finding that they had made disposition of their troops, the Texans then withdrew to their camping place.

The proud Texas general said — in so many words — that his men were most eager to get into the fight as they felt they could whip their weight in wildcats. Even though the enemy had received five hundred additional troops in the night, giving them a superiority in numbers, there was scarcely a single Texan who did not feel that he could lick any four or five Mexicans — even at two to one they felt they had the superiority of fighting ability.

By the time Houston got to the battle he could scarcely dash the words off fast enough. What it

110

amounted to was that his men were very quick to take their positions for the battle; and when it once started they swept in-and-through Santa Anna's army like a Texas tornado ripping across the prairie. It was so vicious and so quick that the battle was over almost by the time it started.

The rest of the day was spent mopping up the fleeing troops and counting the heavy casualties, for the Mexicans had fallen faster than hailstones, covering the ground around the Texans with their motionless forms.

The general applauded his troops for performing day after day in a most magnificent and courageous manner, telling how they overcame such difficulties as bad weather, sickness, short rations and skimpy clothing — always willing themselves to keep going so they could catch Santa Anna and reap full revenge for the atrocities at the Alamo and Goliad.

He particularly mentioned his able officers, singling out Col. Tom Rusk, who proved to be a great leader of men and a fine military strategist. It would be hard to keep from commending the war secretary of the Horseback Government too highly for all that he did in making this effort such a success.

A complete list of all those that took part in the battle was included so that each might be equally honored, since all had performed so excellently. The Texas general concluded the communique by signing his name in bold, egotistical strokes — Sam Houston, Commander in Chief.

Later

Though Sam Houston won the battle, the Horseback Government — under the leadership of David Burnet — won the war. It was now up to the lawmen to perform the thousand and one details to firmly establish Texas as a republic.

Burnet was disturbed more than he cared to admit over not receiving the victory messages sooner. Nevertheless, he calmed down and proceeded with plans — in the thick of the wild jubilation — to go to the battlefield.

Then he sent word for the destitute runaways to return to their homes, many of which had been looted or burned down. It was late for planting but they could still lay by a crop of corn and start their vegetable gardens again, weather permitting.

Lorenzo de Zavala, in the meantime, had heard the news earlier. As soon as he found out about it he knew what he had to do. He hastened to see his former friend and now archenemy — Santa Anna.

It was not easy. Together, the two native-born Mexicans had worked their way to the top, where they became involved in a bitter struggle over political issues. Santa Anna had chosen the side of the rich and the military, while Zavala held fast for the masses and democratic ideals.

Their eyes met. Each, no doubt, thought of many things to say but there was no form to their lips. Finally, Zavala recovered himself with a start. He greeted his once-superior officer, then moved toward him. And they made their peace with each other.

Zavala warned about the great dangers involved. He stressed that he still favored following the rules of human treatment for prisoners — which was so much a part of the real democracy — and that he would do all he could to protect him.

112

The Texas patriot felt at this particular time that his adopted country still needed him in performing this giant task. So he asked to be taken back into the executive family — and he was.

The members of the Horseback Government joined Houston and Rusk on the battlefield. Everything was turned over to Burnet, except the Mexican money — which had already been divided out among the soldiers who had fought in the battle. And the injured general took off shortly for a hospital in New Orleans.

From there on, Burnet took command as the chief government officer. Other cabinet meetings were held at New Washington, Galveston, and Velasco — depending upon the urgency of the situation at hand. A few of the many pressing tasks they had to perform were executing treaties — and there were two, one secret and the other not so secret; disposing of prisoners; aborting another Mexican invasion; ratifying the Constitution, which was framed back in March at the then-capital of Washington-on-the-Brazos; and laying orderly plans for the new government to take over.

Perhaps the most serious and urgent problem was keeping Santa Anna safe while he was waiting to be returned to Mexico. The Texas officials had to cool the heels of newly arrived volunteers from the United States, who were out to get the dictator — come hell or high water. But the courageous men — especially Burnet — stood their ground and prevented an assassination under the most adverse conditions.

It took all summer to bring an assemblance of law and order into being for the fledgling Republic. After seven bruising months the founding fathers felt

113

they had fulfilled their responsibilities as officers of the Horseback (Ad Interim) Government. So they resigned and Sam Houston took over in the fall as president of the Republic of Texas.

Taps had echoed through the new country for brave, fever-ridden Bailey Hardeman in September, as he was placed in his tomb to join the late David Thomas. Lorenzo de Zavala, the brainy, pocket-sized diplomat, passed on in November as the result of a boating accident near his home, which later threw him into pneumonia. Handsome Sam Carson, who continued to fight the fever bout, was the next patriot to pass on two years later.

Tired and worn David Burnet, who was the oldest of the men and incidentally the one who lived the longest, returned to his Oakland home with Hannah and their remaining child to practice law for many years. Tom Rusk, the brash young go-between, returned to his home and law practice in Nacogdoches. Restless, man-of-many-moods Robert Potter put out to sea with the beautiful Harriet Page (or Potter) eventually settling down on Caddo Lake. They all continued to stay active in politics from time to time.

The seven brave and gallant men on horseback were as different from each other as day and night but they had one thing in common. They were determined to have a "free, sovereign, and independent republic" — come what may. Together, they followed through and started THE REPUBLIC OF TEXAS — a nation which was so fabulous that not one of them could have possibly told the extent of its far-flung borders.

REMEMBER THE SEVEN
MEN ON HORSEBACK!

THE SEVEN MEN ON HORSEBACK

TITLE	NAME	BIRTH	MARRIAGE	*	DEATH	BURIED	HONORS
President	David Gouverneur Burnet	New Jersey 4-14, 1788	Hannah Este	4	Galveston 12-5, 1870	State Cemetery	Burnet County Monument on Clarksville High School campus
Vice-Pres.	Lorenzo de Zavala	Yucatan 10-3, 1789	Teresa Correa Emily West	3 3	near Buffalo Bayou 11-15, 1836	near Buffalo Bayou—old de Zavala Cemetery	Zavala County Monument at San Jacinto State Park
Sec. of State	Samuel Price Carson	North Carolina 1-22, 1798	Catherine Wilson	2	Hot Springs, Arkansas 11-2, 1838	unable to locate grave site	Carson County
Sec. of Treasury	Bailey Hardeman	Tennessee 2-26, 1795	Rebecca Wilson	?	Caney Creek Matagorda County 9-25, 1836	State Cemetery	Hardeman County
Sec. of War	Thomas Jefferson Rusk	South Carolina 12-5, 1803	Mary F. Cleveland	7	Nacogdoches 7-29, 1857	Oak Grove Cemetery Nacogdoches	Rusk County Marker at site of home in Nacogdoches Monument on Court House grounds at Henderson
Sec. of Navy	Robert Potter	North Carolina June, 1799	Miss Taylor Harriet Page?	2 3	Caddo Lake 3-2, 1842	State Cemetery	Potter County
Atty. General	David Thomas	Tennessee 1801	Single		On & about 4-19, 1836 aboard *Cayuga*	near Buffalo Bayou—old de Zavala Cemetery	Monument at San Jacinto State Park

* NO. CHILDREN

TEXAS DECLARATION OF INDEPENDENCE

When a government has ceased to protect the lives, liberty and property of the people from whom its legitimate powers are derived, and for the advancement of whose happiness it was instituted, and so far from being a guarantee for the enjoyment of their inestimable and inalienable rights, becomes an instrument in the hands of evil rulers for their oppression; when the Federal Republican Constitution of their country, which they have sworn to support, no longer has a substantial existence, and the whole nature of their government has been forcibly changed without their consent, from a restricted Federative Republic, composed of sovereign states, to a consolidated central military despotism, in which every interest is disregarded but that of the army and the priesthood, both the eternal enemies of civil liberty, the ever ready minions of power and the usual instruments of tyrants; when, long after the spirit of the Constitution has departed, moderation is at length so far lost by those in power, that even the semblance of freedom is removed, and the forms themselves of the Constitution discontinued; and so far from their petitions and remonstrances being regarded, the agents who bear them are thrown into dungeons and mercenary armies sent forth to force a new government upon them at the point of the bayonet; when, in consequence of such acts of malfeasance and abdication on the part of the government, anarchy prevails, and civil society is dissolved into its original elements in such a crisis, the first law of nature, the right of

116

self-preservation, the inherent and inalienable right of the people to appeal to first principles, and take their political affairs into their own hands in extreme cases, enjoins it as a right toward themselves, and a sacred obligation to their posterity, to abolish such government, and create another in its stead, calculated to rescue them from impending dangers, and to secure their future welfare and happiness.

Nations, as well as individuals, are amenable for their acts to the public opinion of mankind. A statement of a part or our grievances is therefore submitted to an impartial world, in justification of the hazardous but unavoidable step now taken, of severing our political connection with the Mexican people, and assuming an independent attitude among the nations of the earth.

The Mexican Government, by its colonization laws invited and induced the Anglo-American population of Texas to colonize its wilderness, under the pledged faith of a written Constitution, that they should continue to enjoy that constitutional liberty and republican government to which they had been habituated in the land of their birth, the United States of America. In this expectation they have been cruelly disappointed, inasmuch as the Mexican Nation has acquiesced in the late changes made in the government by Gen. Antonio Lopez de Santa Anna, who, having overturned the Constitution of his country, now offers us the cruel alternative, either to abandon our homes, acquired by so many privations, or submit to the most intolerable of all tyranny, the combined despotism of the sword and the priesthood.

It hath sacrificed our welfare to the State of Coahuila, by which our interests have been continually depressed, through a jealous and partial course of

117

legislation, carried on at a far-distant seat of government, by a hostile majority, in an unknown tongue; and this, too, notwithstanding we have petitioned in the humblest terms for the establishment of a separate state government, and have, in accordance with the provisions of the National Constitution, presented to the General Congress, a Republican Constitution, which was without just cause, contemptuously rejected.

It incarcerated in a dungeon, for a long time, one of our citizens, for no other cause but a zealous endeavor to procure the acceptance of our Constitution and the establishment of a state government.

It has failed and refused to secure, on a firm basis, the right of trial by jury, that palladium of civil liberty and only safe guarantee for the life, liberty and property of the citizen.

It has failed to establish any public system of education, although possessed of almost boundless resources (the public domain), and although it is an axiom in political science that, unless a people are educated and enlightened, it is idle to expect the continuance of civil liberty, or the capacity for self-government.

It has suffered the military commandants stationed among us to exercise arbitrary acts of oppression and tyranny, thus trampling upon the most sacred rights of the citizen, and rendering the military superior to the civil power.

It has dissolved by force of arms the State Congress of Coahuila and Texas, and obliged our representatives to fly for their lives from the seat of government, thus depriving us of the fundamental political right of representation.

It has demanded the surrender of a number of

our citizens, and ordered military detachments to seize and carry them into the interior for trial, in contempt of the civil authorities, and in defiance of the laws and the Constitution.

It has made piratical attacks upon our commerce by commissioning foreign desperadoes, and authorizing them to seize our vessels and convey the property of our citizens to far-distant ports for confiscation.

It denies us the right of worshiping the Almighty according to the dictates of our own consciences, by the support of a national religion calculated to promote the temporal interests of its human functionaries rather than the glory of the true and living God.

It has demanded us to deliver up our arms, which are essential to our defense, the rightful property of freemen, and formidable only to tyrannical governments.

It has invaded our country, both by sea and by land, with intent to lay waste our territory, and drive us from our homes; and has now a large mercenary army advancing to carry on against us a war of extermination.

It has, through its emissaries, incited the merciless savage, with the tomahawk and scalping knife, to massacre the inhabitants of our defenseless frontiers.

It has been, during the whole time of our connection with it, the contemptible sport and victim of successive military revolutions, and hath continually exhibited every characteristic of a weak, corrupt and tyrannical government.

These and other grievances were patiently borne by the people of Texas, until they reached that point at which forbearance ceases to be a virtue. They then took up arms in defense of the National Constitution. They appealed to their Mexican brethren for assistance. Their appeal has been made in vain; though months have elapsed, no sympathetic response has yet been heard from the interior. They are, therefore, forced to the melancholy conclusion that the Mexican people have acquiesced in the destruction of their liberty, and the substitution therefore of a military despotism; that they are unfit to be free, and incapable of self-government.

The necessity of self-preservation, therefore, now decrees our eternal political separation.

We, therefore, the delegates, with plenary powers, of the people of Texas, in solemn convention assembled, appealing to a candid world for the necessities of our condition, do hereby resolve and declare that our political connection with the Mexican nation has forever ended, and that the people of Texas do now constitute a free, sovereign and independent Republic, and are fully invested with all the rights and attributes which properly belong to independent states; and, conscious of the rectitude of our intentions, we fearlessly and confidently commit the issue to the decision of the Supreme Arbiter of the destinies of nations.

S I G N E R S :

Richard Ellis, President

Charles B. Stewart
Thomas Barnett
James Collinsworth
Edwin Waller
John S. D. Byrom
Francisco Ruiz
José Antonio Navarro
Jessie B. Badgett
William D. Lacey
William Menifee
John Fisher
Mathew Caldwell
J. William Mottley
Lorenzo de Zavala
Stephen H. Everitt
George W. Smyth
Elijah Stapp
Claiborne West
William B. Scates
M. B. Menard
A. B. Hardin
J. W. Bunton
Thomas J. Gazley
R. M. Coleman
Sterling C. Robertson
George C. Childress
Bailey Hardeman
Robert Potter
Thomas Jefferson Rusk

Charles S. Taylor
John S. Roberts
Robert Hamilton
Collin McKinney
Albert H. Latimer
James Power
Sam Houston
David Thomas
Edward Conrad
Martin Parmer
Edward O. LeGrand
Stephen W. Blount
James Gaines
William Clark Jr.
Sydney O. Pennington
William Carroll Crawford
John Turner
Benjamin B. Goodrich
G. W. Barnett
James G. Swisher
Jesse Grimes
S. Rhoads Fisher
John W. Moore
John W. Bower
Samuel A. Maverick
Sam P. Carson
A. Briscoe
James B. Woods
Asa Brigham

121

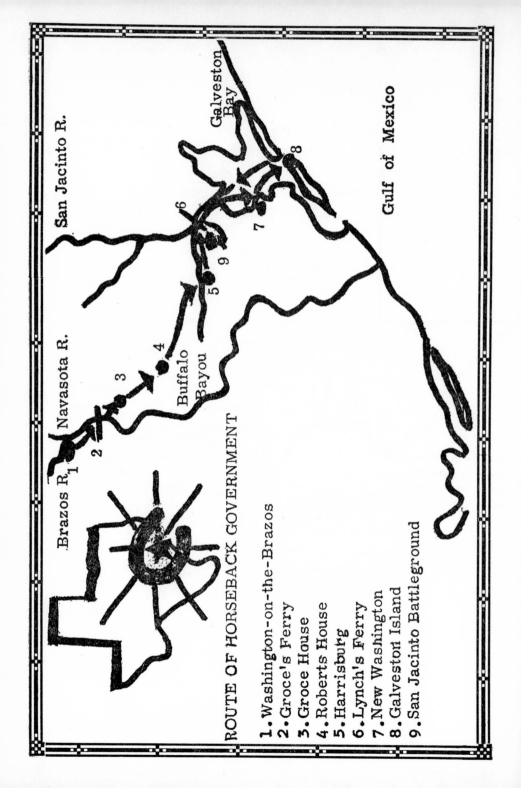

ROUTE OF HORSEBACK GOVERNMENT

1. Washington-on-the-Brazos
2. Groce's Ferry
3. Groce House
4. Roberts House
5. Harrisburg
6. Lynch's Ferry
7. New Washington
8. Galveston Island
9. San Jacinto Battleground

Brazos R.
Navasota R.
San Jacinto R.
Buffalo Bayou
Galveston Bay
Gulf of Mexico

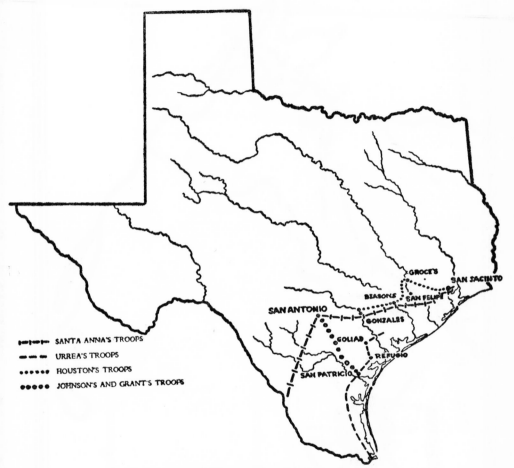

SANTA ANNA'S TROOPS
URREA'S TROOPS
HOUSTON'S TROOPS
JOHNSON'S AND GRANT'S TROOPS

GROCE'S
SAN JACINTO
BEASON'S
SAN FELIPE
SAN ANTONIO
GONZALES
GOLIAD
REFUGIO
SAN PATRICIO

Routes of Troops in the Revolution

From *Texas: Wilderness to Space Age* by Pool, Elliott, and **Raley**, published by **The** Naylor Company

BIBLIOGRAPHY

Unpublished Materials

Chambless, Beauford. *The Ad-Interim Government of the Republic of Texas.* Thesis presented to the faculty of the Graduate Department of the Rice Institute in partial fulfillment of the requirements for the degree of Master of Arts, Houston, Texas, June, 1949.

Chambless, Beauford. *The First President of the Republic of Texas: The Life of David Gouverneur Burnet.* Thesis submitted to the faculty of the Graduate Department of the Rice Institute in partial fulfillment of the requirements for the degree of Doctor of Philosophy, Houston, Texas, June, 1954.

Mosley, Huey Floyd. *The Ad Interim Government of Texas: March 17 to October 22, 1836.* Thesis, East Texas State College, submitted in partial fulfillment of the requirements for the degree of Master of Arts, Commerce, Texas, August, 1939.

124

Sloan, Sallie Everett. *The Presidential Administra-tion of David G. Burnet, March 17-October 22, 1836.* Thesis for Master of Arts, The Univer-sity of Texas, Austin, Texas, June, 1918.

Putman, Lucile. *Washington-on-the-Brazos.* East Texas State Teacher's College, submitted in partial fulfillment of the requirements for the degree of Master of Arts, Commerce, Texas, August, 1952.

Periodicals

Barker, Eugene C. "Land Speculation as a Cause of the Texas Revolution." *Texas Historical As-sociation Quarterly.* Vol. X, July, 1906.

——. "President Jackson and the Texas Revolution." *American Historical Review.* Vol. XII, July, 1907.

——. "The San Jacinto Campaign." *Texas Historical Association Quarterly.* Vol. IV, April, 1901.

——. "The Texan Revolutionary Army." *Texas His-torical Association Quarterly.* Vol. IX, April, 1906.

Beazley, Julia. "Letters and Documents: David G. Burnet." *Southwestern Historical Quarterly.* Vol. XLIV, October, 1940.

Blount, Lois Foster. "A Brief Study of Thomas J. Rusk Based on His Letters to His Brother, David, 1835-1856." *Southwestern Historical Quarterly.* Vol. XXXIV, April, 1931.

Boyle, Andrew A. "Reminiscences of the Texas Rev-olution." *Texas Historical Association Quarter-ly.* Vol. XIII, April, 1910.

Cleaves, W. S. "Lorenzo de Zavala in Texas." *South-western Historical Quarterly.* Vol. XXXVI, July, 1932.

Dienst, Alexander. "The Navy of the Republic of Texas, I." *Texas Historical Association Quarterly*. Vol. XII, January, 1909.

——. "The Navy of the Republic of Texas, II." *Texas Historical Association Quarterly*. Vol. XII, April, 1909.

Estep, Raymond. "Lorenzo de Zavala and the Texas Revolution." *Southwestern Historical Quarterly*. Vol. LVII, January, 1954.

Fields, Dorothy Louise. "David Gouverneur Burnet." *Southwestern Historical Quarterly*. Vol. XLIX, October, 1945.

Fulmore, Z. T. "Samuel Price Carson." *Texas Historical Association Quarterly*. Vol. VIII, January, 1905.

Geiser, S. W. "David Gouverneur Burnet, Satirist." *Southwestern Historical Quarterly*. Vol. XLVIII, July, 1955.

Henderson, H. M. "A Critical Analysis of the San Jacinto Campaign." *Southwestern Historical Quarterly*. Vol. LIX, January, 1956.

Jones, Billy M. "Health Seekers in Early Anglo-American Texas." *Southwestern Historical Quarterly*. Vol. LXIX, January, 1966.

Jones, Pauline H. and Robert L. "Samuel Price Carson." *Texana*. Vol. 6, Fall, 1968.

Ledbetter, Nan Thompson. "The Muddy Brazos in Early Texas." *Southwestern Historical Quarterly*. Vol. LXIII, October, 1959.

Looscan, Adele B. "Harris County 1822-1845." *Southwestern Historical Quarterly*. Vol. XVIII, October, 1914.

McDonald, Archie P. "The Young Men of the Texas Revolution." *Texana*. Vol. 3, Winter, 1965.

Muir, Andrew Forest. "The Municipality of Harrisburg, 1835-1836." *Southwestern Historical Quarterly.* Vol. LVI, July, 1952.

Norvell, James R. "The Ames Case Revisited." *Southwestern Historical Quarterly.* Vol. LXIII, July, 1959.

Rowland, Kate Mason. "General John Thomson Mason." *The Quarterly.* Vol. XI, January, 1908.

Shuffler, R. Henderson. "Notes and Documents, The Ark of the Covenant of the Texas Declaration of Independence." *Southwestern Historical Quarterly. Vol.* LXV, July, 1961.

——. "The Signing of Texas' Declaration of Independence: Myth and Record." *Southwestern Historical Quarterly.* Vol. LXV, January, 1962.

Simmons, Marc S. "Notes and Documents: Samuel T. Allen and the Texas Revolution." *Southwestern Historical Quarterly.* Vol. LXVIII, April, 1965.

Singletary, Otis A. "Book Reviews." *Southwestern Historical Quarterly,* Vol. LXIII, July, 1959.

Sternberg, Richard R. "Jackson's Neches Claim, 1829-1836." *Southwestern Historical Quarterly.* Vol. XXXIX, April, 1936.

Todd, Gary. "Historic Park Series: Washington-on-the-Brazos, Eighteen Days of Valor." *Texas Parks and Wildlife.* January, 1966.

Weber, Josie. "The Town of Washington." *Texas Magazine.* February, 15, 1970.

Books

Barker, Eugene Campbell. *Mexico and Texas.* Dallas: P. L. Turner Company, 1928.

Binkley, William Campbell. *The Texas Revolution.*

Baton Rouge: Louisiana State University Press, 1952.

Day, James M. *Texas Almanac 1857-1873*. Waco: Texian Press, 1967.

DeShields, James T. *They Sat in High Places*. San Antonio: The Naylor Company, 1940.

Dobie, James Frank. *In the Shadow of History*. Hatboro: Folk-lore Associates, 1966.

Garner, Claud W. *Sam Houston: Texas Giant*. San Antonio: The Naylor Company, 1969.

Gilbert, Charles E., Jr. *A Concise History of Early Texas*. Houston: Adco Press, Incorporated, 1964.

Gray, Col. William F. *Diary of Col. Wm. F. Gray*. Houston: The Fletcher Young Publishing Company, 1965.

Hobby, A. M. *Life and Times of David G. Burnet*. Galveston: Steam Book and Job Office of Galveston News, 1871.

Holley, Mary Austin. *Texas*. Austin: The Steck Company, 1935.

Kemp, Louis Wiltz. *The Signers of the Texas Declaration of Independence*. Houston: The Anson Jones Press, 1944.

Leclerc, Frédéric. *Texas and Its Revolution*. Houston: A. Jones Press, 1950.

Mitchell, O. O., Jr. *Texas History Movies*. Austin: Graphic Ideas, Incorporated, 1970.

Newell, Rev. Chester. *History of the Revolution in Texas*. Austin: The Steck Company, 1935.

Rickard, J. A. *Famous Politicians*. Dallas: Upshaw and Company, 1955.

Santa Anna, Antonio López de. *The Mexican Side of the Revolution*. Dallas: P. L. Turner Company, 1928.

Shearer, Ernest C. *Robert Potter: Remarkable North Carolinian and Texan.* Houston: University of Houston Press, 1951.

Steen, Ralph W. *History of Texas.* Austin: The Steck Company, 1939.

Vigness, David M. *The Revolutionary Decades.* Austin: Steck-Vaughn Company, 1965.

Wallace, Ernest and Vigness, David M. *Documents of Texas History.* Austin: The Steck Company, 1963.

Webb, Walter Prescott. Editor. *The Handbook of Texas.* Austin: The Texas State Historical Association, 1952, 2 vols.

Yoakum, H., Esq. *History of Texas.* Austin: The Steck Company, 1959.

Manuscript Collections

The Archives of The Texas State Library
    Convention Papers
    Domestic Correspondence
    Financial Affairs Papers
    Proclamation Papers

Newspapers

The Eugene C. Barker Library of The University of Texas
    The *Telegraph* and *Texas Register*

Stephenson, Mrs. Charles. "Honeymoon Boat to Texas." *Dallas News,* December 4, 1927.